STORY™

by Joe Schreiber

Based on the screenplay by
Jonathan Kasdan & Lawrence Kasdan

D·ISNEY
LUCASFILM
P R E S S

Los Angeles • New York

First Edition, September 2018
1 3 5 7 9 10 8 6 4 2
FAC-025438-18212

Library of Congress Control Number on file
ISBN 978-1-368-04493-6

Visit www.starwars.com

SUSTAINABLE
FORESTRY
INITIATIVE

Certified Chain of Custody
Promoting Sustainable Forestry

www.sfiprogram.org
SFI-01054

The SFI label applies to the text stock

A long time ago in a galaxy far,
far away....

CHAPTER 1

THE NIGHT HAD EYES.

Somewhere over Narro Sienar Boulevard, the searchlight from an Imperial patrol bike scanned the blackness, cutting through clouds of exhaust and industrial pollution in search of trouble. The kid ducked the surveillance with instinctive ease, cut left around a corner, and vanished into shadow. The gang would be looking for him three blocks away, under the overpass where the deal had gone sour. All the kid had to do was keep them guessing, and he had no problem with that. He'd been outwitting lower life-forms all his life, as a matter of self-preservation.

His name was Han, and he liked to steal things.

Behind him, warehouses and tenements rose into the night, their outlines carving darkened shapes against the wider cityscape. Sirens sounded in the distance, but Han hardly heard them. Having grown up there, in the alleyways and shipyards of Corellia, he'd long before gotten used to the smells and sounds of the city. It was home.

Somewhere above him, the searchlight swung back around, the patrol bike prowling closer for a second pass, but it didn't matter. Han had already found what he'd gone looking for.

The M-68 landspeeder was exactly where he'd seen it earlier, an irresistible temptation just waiting for the right set of hands to coax it to life and claim it. In one fluid motion he moved up alongside it, crouched down, and slipped underneath. Gloves on and tools out, penlight clamped in his teeth, he worked fast, rewiring the speeder's alarm system and bypassing its security mechanisms.

Thirty seconds later he was jumping into the front seat, popping the panel off the steering column to get at the starter and battery wires. Sparks flew as he stripped the wires, wrapped them together, and tapped the starter.

He sat there for a moment, listening to the speeder's repulsorlift engine roar to life. His face was caked in soot and ash, nose bleeding freely and left eye starting to bruise from the beating they'd thrown him down at the docks, but those injuries were already forgotten. Behind the wheel he felt reborn, as fresh and alive as he'd ever felt in his entire life.

A cockeyed smile curved his mouth. Reaching into his pocket, he pulled out a pair of aurodium-plated gold dice and hung them from the speeder's rearview mirror. To the kid's eye, they looked just right, a promise of something better just around the corner. Good luck? Fortune and glory?

Whatever it is, he thought, *I'll take it.*

For a kid like Han, around eighteen and chasing whatever dream might get him off that cesspool of a planet, a boosted speeder and pair of cheap golden dice just might be enough to send him on his way.

Seconds later he was blasting down Narro Sienar Boulevard at a velocity that felt just short of lightspeed. His chest tightened, a familiar feeling of anticipation building inside him, a sense of freedom beckoning him onward.

Up ahead, the road forked, and off to the left he could already see the gleaming promise of Coronet Spaceport, where huge passenger liners were waiting to head out to distant systems. Off to the right, the road veered into the grubby industrial thickets of the Corellian slums, crumbling tenements housing the desperate and downtrodden—people like . . . well, like him.

Torn, Han glanced at the golden dice, then at the empty seat beside him. Qi'ra belonged there, and they both knew it.

He wasn't leaving without her.

Decision made, he shot across the road, taking the right fork into the slum and, for better or worse, toward home.

For the lost souls who'd grown up there, the Den of the White Worms was a grimy sanctuary from a squalid world, a place where they might be slightly safer from their enemies—if their friends didn't kill them first. Han wasn't out of the speeder before he heard the snarling of the Sibian hounds just inside the door. The hounds weighed up to a hundred kilos, and were all teeth, jaw, and muscle. Any of the scrumrats who lived in the Den could depend on the hounds to defend their turf from outsiders. Whether or not they let Han live after he talked to Lady Proxima remained to be seen.

"Han!" someone called out. Glancing up, he saw two of the older White Worms, Cosdra and LeKelf, perched near the entrance of the Den. Proxima had rewarded their loyalty with the opportunity to serve as sentries, watching for arrivals and departures while enjoying air that was a little fresher than what was below the surface.

"What happened to your face?" Cosdra asked, his tone more suspicious than concerned.

Han waved it away. "Minor misunderstanding." Slipping through the cluttered doorway and past the hounds, he heard the scrumrats murmuring around him, comparing the day's haul of booty they'd managed to snag from unwitting victims. Jewelry, credits, articles of clothing, silk scarves, or bags—nothing was too big or too small to be stolen and taken before Lady Proxima for her personal assessment.

Han took a breath and waited for his eyes to adjust to the gloom. How many more times was he supposed to return to that dump before he finally put it in his rearview mirror? Making his way through the labyrinth of vermin-infested tunnels and hallways, he pushed past scrumrats hunched over their ill-gotten gains, some throwing dice and gambling with gyroballs while others literally played with fire, squirting petrol into burn barrels and cackling hysterically as the glow of the flames flickered over their faces.

The White Worms weren't exactly friends, more like

fellow soldiers in a war of poverty and exploitation that never seemed to end. Dodging the authorities, doing whatever was necessary to stay alive, they had honed the art of self-preservation in a world that didn't care whether they lived or died.

They had come from different backgrounds but shared the common thread of hardship, which forced them to do whatever was necessary to survive. Young thieves like Hallon and Tunnel Toli had either lost their parents or simply never known them, and the community they'd forged there, for better or worse, was home. Then there was Bansee, a mean-spirited, humorless older girl who had caught Lady Proxima's attention because of her talent with the pipe she called a "rat hammer"—a weapon that she didn't hesitate to use on anyone who displeased her. The thief called Chates had been a farmer's son who'd accompanied his father to Coronet one day. Muggers had murdered the old man while he'd been visiting a bank, leaving Chates an orphan alone in the city, where he'd fallen in with the scrumrats.

Han made his way deeper into the tunnel. Rumor had it that the Den had once been a manufacturing plant, and some of the old machinery had been left behind to rust, silent and ominous, in distant corners, like the ghosts of failed industry. The unreliable electricity and lights that still functioned down there were the work of the Den's resident genius, Han's now-deceased friend Tsuulo, who before he died had managed to tap into the power grid of a nearby factory so they could keep some of the power on, some of the time.

Han walked faster but stepped carefully, aware as always that the darkness around him was alive and squirming. It was no coincidence that Bansee's rat-hunting skills had promoted her to the position of Third Girl. The Den was infested with vervikks, screerats, and other unwholesome vermin, and he and the other Worms were tasked with hunting them and taking them to Proxima's pools, where she chewed them up and fed them to her baby worms.

Approaching the heat of the furnace, he could make out the shapes of young bodies asleep on the floor or piled into hammocks and cots, exhausted by fear and the sheer ugly brutality of life. He stepped around them with an agility borne of long experience, his eyes already adjusted to the darkness. Rounding the corner, he felt an arm reach out, the figure emerging from the shadows to draw him close to her.

"Qi'ra," he said, and grinned as she drew him to her and pressed her lips to his. At eighteen, she was Proxima's Head Girl—confident, quick thinking, and just about the only thing in the Den that Han valued above his own existence. There amid the squalor and the stench, a stolen kiss from her was a minor miracle he would gladly have stopped time, at least for a while, to keep enjoying a little longer.

Qi'ra drew back and looked up at him, taking in the injuries on his face. "You were gone too long today. I knew something must've gone wrong."

"This? Is nothing. You should see them." Han drew her closer. "Actually, they're fine."

"What happened?"

"In the middle of the exchange, I'm handing over the coaxium when his goons jumped me. But I showed 'em."

Qi'ra raised an eyebrow. "Yeah? How?"

"I ran away. Then I boosted their speeder. You're gonna love it."

"We going somewhere?"

"Yeah. Anywhere you want." Reaching into his pocket, he drew out the small metal cylinder containing a tiny nugget of coaxium. Qi'ra stared at it, immediately recognizing what it meant.

"You held on to one of the vials! This is worth—"

"Five, six hundred credits." Han nodded. "More than you said we'd need."

"To buy our way out of the Control Zone and off Corellia. Han, this could work!"

"This is gonna work," Han said. "Qi'ra, you always said one day we were gonna get out of here. This is it."

"What are we waiting for?" Qi'ra asked.

Han was about to answer when a rough hand grabbed him and jerked him backward so hard that his teeth snapped together. Spinning, he found himself face to face with a twisted, acne-scarred face as the bigger kid slammed him into the wall.

"Hey, Rebolt," Han said, and felt another, far worse

presence materializing. A cloaked albino face appeared out of the blackness. "And Moloch. Good to see you guys. What a night I had. I mean, you're not gonna believe it. You'll believe it, but—"

Moloch glared at him, the hideous pallor of his face radiating cold hatred. Instead of Basic, he spoke a language Han only recognized from years of having to listen to it barking orders and making threats. "You're late. And Lady Proxima does not like to be kept waiting."

"I was *just* going to see her."

"We'll make sure that you don't get lost along the way."

It was oppressively dark, the smell of raw sewage so heavy that Han had to breathe through his mouth to keep from gagging. He'd never gotten used to that smell, no matter how many times he'd gone in there. Shapes moved in the blackness—other scrumrats huddled nearby on the floor. All the windows had been painted black to keep out the light. Outside the Den, dawn was coming, daylight creeping across the tenements as if apprehensive of what it might find. But in there, Proxima needed it dark, very dark, to protect her delicate skin and the skin of her babies.

From the pool in front of him, the thick white worm creature emerged slowly into view with a splash, skin oozing through the steel ringlets that adorned her like jeweled armor as she rose to her full height, towering over Han. He tried to smile, but it didn't work as well as he'd hoped.

"Well?" Lady Proxima asked. "What happened?"

"They double-crossed you, tried to kill me."

She gazed at him for a moment. "The money?"

"They kept it."

"And . . ." She lowered her head, drawing close enough that he could smell the sour, rotten warmth of her breath. "My coaxium?"

"Kept that, too." He straightened up a bit, cocking his head. "But hey, I think we all learned a valuable lesson. We cannot trust those guys."

"So you expect me to believe you walked away with nothing?" Lady Proxima asked.

"Well, I ran away with my life. I think that's something," Han pointed out.

Lady Proxima looked at him. "I trusted you with a simple task and all I'm hearing are excuses."

"Hey, take it easy, I wasn't—"

THWACK! Han felt a bright explosion of pain in his stomach. Doubling over with a gasp, barely keeping his footing, he saw through watering eyes as Rebolt swung the expandable baton and slammed it harder into his gut. His legs abandoned him entirely, and he fell to the floor. Dimly, as if from some great distance, he was aware of Lady Proxima's voice as she addressed the other scrumrats in the room.

"Pay attention, children. Learn from Han's mistake. I will give you everything I have, all my love, and all I ask in return is obedience and loyalty. But there must be repercussions for failure, or else you . . . never . . . learn."

Han managed to raise his head. His heart was pounding

and his ribs ached when he breathed. Yet somehow he looked up, met her gaze, and spoke.

"You know what? I don't think I'm ever gonna learn."

Lady Proxima's eyes blazed, abruptly furious. "What did you say?"

Rebolt swung the baton again, but this time Han reached out and caught it, yanking it from Rebolt's hand, flipping it around, and pointing it directly at the other boy's face. For a moment, the stunned expression on that cruel face was the most glorious thing Han had ever seen. He started to grin again. He couldn't help it.

"Next time somebody hits me, I'm gonna hit back."

Lady Proxima's eyes boiled with fury at the expression of defiance. Then her attention flicked to something next to Han, and Han saw Moloch step from the shadows with something in his hand. Han knew what it was—a snub-nosed double-barreled blaster with a scope atop it, both barrels pointed directly at his head.

"I wonder, boy," Moloch sneered, "what will you do when I shoot you."

It wasn't really a question, only a simple statement of fact. Han was aware that Moloch's finger was already tightening on the trigger, and he slipped his hand into his pocket, opening his mouth to speak.

But the next words that were spoken were not in his voice at all.

"Moloch," Qi'ra said, "don't shoot. Please."

Turning, he saw her step toward them, moving directly in front of Moloch's blaster. Her voice was soft, reasonable, but she seemed well aware of what she was risking by stepping in front of the weapon. Han's smile returned.

She flashed him a warning glance, but Moloch had already begun to lower his blaster.

"Qi'ra," Lady Proxima said, "you poor, misguided thing. Remember what we saved you from. Remember the Silo. We pulled you out of that horror, gave you a home and protection. Shelter from the storm. Don't throw it away for Han. He's not worth it."

Qi'ra made the slightest shrug, as if to say, *Maybe not*. "But he's worth more alive than dead. Whatever he lost in the deal, we'll make it back. Double! We'll make it up to you."

"Twenty-two thousand."

Qi'ra recoiled, stunned. "Seriously? Twenty-two *thousand*?"

"I told you it didn't go well," Han said.

"I should've let them kill you."

"Too late for haggling," Lady Proxima said. "I have no choice but to kill him. Maybe I'll sell you. You may still be worth a few credits." Then, with a perfunctory nod at Moloch: "All right, go ahead."

Moloch raised the blaster again, eyes trained on Qi'ra. "You'll never know how much it pains me to destroy something as beautiful as you."

"Everybody stand back." Han pulled a spherical object

from his pocket, holding it up at arm's length. Instinctively, everybody jumped back, with the exception of Lady Proxima, whose lips curled into a hideous parody of a grin.

"What's that supposed to be?"

"This? It's a thermal detonator." He tightened his grip, sliding his thumb up the side. "That I just armed."

Lady Proxima's mocking expression didn't change. "It's a rock."

"No, it's not."

"Yes, it is." Her eyes, able to see perfectly in the dark, narrowed ever so slightly. "You just made a clicking sound with your mouth."

Qi'ra let out a small breath, speaking to Han just above a whisper. "Tell me this wasn't your plan."

"No," he said, "this is."

And with that, he threw the rock at the window behind them, the dark glass shattering into a thousand shards and letting in a sudden spray of light.

That was when the screaming started.

CHAPTER 2

"WAS *THIS* YOUR PLAN?"

They were roaring down the narrow backstreets of Corellia in the boosted M-68 speeder, Han behind the wheel and Qi'ra next to him, gripping the console in front of her as the wind blew back her hair. She'd never looked more beautiful, or more wild. Somewhere behind them, the White Worm goons were in pursuit, Moloch's speeder truck surging closer, with the Sibian hounds loaded in the back. But the element of surprise—the few crucial seconds Han had bought them as Lady Proxima shrieked and writhed while daylight assaulted her delicate skin—had gotten them out of there with enough of a lead that an almost impossible hope had sprung up in his heart. Maybe it was just the fact that Qi'ra was with him, smiling and hopeful, with those ridiculous golden dice dangling in front of them, the promise of freedom not so far away.

"There's a starliner leaving from Coronet Spaceport," he said. "We're gonna be on it."

Qi'ra slipped her hand into Han's pocket and held up the vial of coaxium. "This'll have to be enough to get us through the Imperial checkpoint without ID chips."

"Are you kidding?" Han smirked. "That's grade A refined coaxium, worth at least seven hundred credits."

"You said five or six."

"Eh." He shrugged. "Once we're through, we're free. I'm gonna be a pilot."

"We get our own ship," Qi'ra said. '

"See the galaxy. All of it."

"Go anywhere we want, and never have to take orders from anybody." She glanced behind her. "But first we have to get clear of Moloch."

"I got this," Han said. They blew past the entrance to a seafront industrial complex, swerving around the security droid and flying past an Imperial patrol bike in a blur. An instant later, the patrol trooper on the speeder bike switched on its lights and gave chase.

"We've got company," Qi'ra said, and then clarified: "More company."

"Hang on." Han fishtailed into an alleyway, swerving around a dilapidated stack of shipping pallets that the patrol bike wasn't agile enough to negotiate. When Qi'ra glanced back again, she saw the patrol trooper wiping out spectacularly, skidding across the asphalt behind them.

"You're pretty good." She grinned. "Done this before?"

"Once or twice—"

THUNK! The speeder jolted forward as Moloch's truck rammed them from behind.

Han shook his head in disbelief. "This guy has no skills, no instincts whatsoever." Angling toward a narrow stretch of alley with the wall on the right side and the Star Destroyer superstructure on the left, he saw the alleyway becoming steadily more narrow, and the idea burst into his mind, fully formed.

"Oh, no." Qi'ra simultaneously realized what he was planning and saw that it was impossible. "We're not gonna make it."

Han pushed the throttle down. "Show a little faith, will ya?"

"I'm telling you, it's too tight."

"For Moloch's speeder truck, yeah. Not for us."

"No, I'm pretty sure it's gonna be too tight for us, too," she said.

"Watch this." At the last possible second, he tilted the speeder sideways to fit it through the narrow gap, scraping the walls on either side. It almost worked. But with a screech of tortured metal, the speeder ground to a halt, wedged at an angle. The repulsorlifts gave out, and the speeder slumped into place with the resigned groan of a machine whose operator had asked it to do the impossible.

"Come on," he said as they unbuckled their harnesses and hit the ground. He grabbed the dice from the rearview mirror. "From here we go by foot."

Three minutes later, they were running through the complex in the opposite direction, and Qi'ra glanced over her shoulder. "Moloch's gonna have the hounds after us if he doesn't already," she said. "We have to throw him off the scent."

"What's the plan?" Han said, and sniffed the air. "And what's that smell?"

"*That's* the plan." She pointed past a busy loading dock filled with nets, pots, and barrels, where exotic seafood was being weighed and gutted by workers wearing rubber boots and aprons. Leaning forward, Qi'ra reached over and yanked the lid off the nearest barrel, and Han looked in to see dark, disgusting shapes wriggling and squirming in the water. *Lots* of dark, disgusting shapes.

"That's . . ." He stopped and swallowed hard. "Are those eels?"

"Get in," Qi'ra said. "Trust me."

He hesitated and heard snarling and barking getting louder in the distance. Eels were bad. The hounds were worse. Reluctantly, with the air of a man who'd done the math and was choosing the lesser of two evils, Han started to lower himself into the barrel.

"Mmm," he said. "Eels are . . . not my favorite."

"You're not alone."

"Eels aren't your favorite, either?"

"No, I mean you won't be alone in the barrel." Climbing in with him, she crouched down, submerging herself to the neck, and drew the lid on top of them. A moment later, under the water, Han felt something press against his leg, sliding closer.

"Did you just touch my thigh?"

Qi'ra shook her head. "That wasn't me."

"Great. You know what, maybe—"

"Shhh!"

They heard the hounds snarling and sniffing just outside the barrel, and then Rebolt himself, sounding disgusted at this turn of events: "Stinks like fleek and scalefin. It's throwing off the scent."

Moloch made a snarling noise, replying in his own language: "They aren't here. Keep moving."

As the noises of the hounds gradually began to diminish, Han looked at Qi'ra. It was dark in there, but she was still close enough that he could see the faint gleam of her eyes gazing back at him. He grinned.

"What?" she said.

"You look beautiful," he said, leaning closer to her, "even surrounded by live eels."

She drew back. "Wait, are you actually going in to kiss me?"

"Just seizing the moment."

"This *isn't* the moment." Pushing him away, she knocked the top off the barrel and leapt out, and Han quickly followed, shrugging it off.

It had been worth a try.

The various terminals and walkways of the spaceport were teeming with travelers of all species, emigrants evading the Empire's ever-tightening grip, getting out while they could. Moving among them, holding Qi'ra's hand, Han felt the two of them disappearing into the greater crowd of hurried passengers.

This is going to work, he thought, slightly amazed at himself. *It's* already *working.*

As if reading his thoughts, Qi'ra drew back a bit. Up ahead, an Imperial immigration checkpoint stood imposingly, a series of control booths staffed by gray-and-black-uniformed emigration officials in black caps. On the far side of the glass barrier, Han could practically see their future waiting for them, a future filled with the promise of freedom, wealth, and untold adventure. It was everything they'd dreamed of, close enough to touch.

"We're almost there," he said. "Just hold on to me and don't look back."

Qi'ra was already focused on the challenge ahead, thinking it through. "Once we're through, we gotta be smart, figure out where we're going."

"Anywhere the Empire isn't. Wherever we go, couldn't be worse than where we've been."

She shook her head. "Yes, it can. Out there we've got no protection. We could get snatched up by traffickers, sold to Crimson Dawn or the Hutt Cartel."

He met her gaze. "Not gonna happen. I won't let it. We'll have each other." He placed something in her hand, and she looked down at the gold dice.

"For luck?"

Han gave her a quick nod and looked up. They reached the front of the line, where the female official was already sizing them up behind the glass. "ID chips."

"Funny story," Han said, "we don't have 'em. But"—he held the vial of glowing fluid just high enough for the official to see it—"we do have this."

"It's worth at least eight hundred credits," Qi'ra said, "maybe more."

"You could be detained just for having that," the official said, but her eyes were riveted to the vial, seemingly in spite of herself.

"What good would that do anybody?" Han asked. "Let us through, and it's all yours."

At first she didn't speak, didn't even move. Then, finally, she tapped the button to extend a metal drawer. "The coaxium. Now."

"No," Qi'ra said firmly. "As we're going through, not before."

Ultimately, though, she saw the official wasn't going to yield. Qi'ra placed the coaxium in the drawer and watched as the official opened the barrier. Han stepped forward through the gateway that led to the starliner. Then, incredibly, he was through, free and clear. Behind him, Qi'ra moved to follow—

—when a hand fell on her shoulder, jerking her backward.

"Going somewhere?"

Han froze. The emigration official's eyes widened at the sight of Rebolt and the other White Worm goons swarming around Qi'ra, grabbing her arms. Instantly, the official hit the alarm, slamming the gate shut, and from his side of the barrier, Han saw them pulling Qi'ra away, dragging her backward. Everything seemed to be happening in slow motion, every detail of the moment enhanced to a terrible degree of clarity. Han felt something break open inside him, a jagged eruption of helpless pain that made Rebolt's baton feel like a faint poke by comparison.

"No!" he shouted. *"Let her go!"*

From the other side of the glass, centimeters away, Qi'ra's eyes met his, and he saw the resignation there. Already she'd realized the outcome was settled.

"Han." The words flew out in a final burst. "Go! Now!"

"I'll come back!" he shouted. "I will! I'll come back!"

Even as they hauled her away, as she disappeared among the goons who'd come to drag her back to the Den, his feet refused to obey. It wasn't until the stormtroopers stationed along the gateway started toward him that the spell was broken and he realized what he needed to do. Forcing himself to move in the opposite direction, his throat aching and his chest on fire with words he hadn't spoken, he turned away and broke into a desperate, directionless run.

No, he amended a moment later, *not quite directionless*.

There was still one avenue open to him, and he meant to take it.

"This is where I sign up to be a pilot, right?" Han asked the Imperial recruiter behind the desk.

"If you apply for the Imperial Navy," the man said, "but most recruits go into the infantry—"

Han forced himself to take a slow, steady breath. After sprinting headlong through the terminal, narrowly avoiding the port's security detail, he stood at the front of the line, still slightly dazed and out of breath. Never had he imagined himself there, yet there he was: "I'm gonna be a pilot," Han insisted, and speaking the words aloud, he realized almost immediately that they were true. "Best in the galaxy. How long will that take?"

"Depends on how good you are at following orders. Why? You have somewhere to be?"

"Yeah. Back here. As soon as I can."

"Don't hear that much," the recruiter said with a shake of his head. "So . . . what's your name?"

"Han."

"Han. Han what?" The recruiter gazed at him impatiently, eyebrows raised, fingers poised over the keypad to complete the application form. "Who are your people?"

Glancing over his shoulder, Han cast one last look at the world he was leaving behind. And Qi'ra. That final image of her—her face on the other side of the glass, her voice giving him permission to leave as Rebolt and the others pulled her away from him—would be burned into his brain forever.

He looked back at the recruiter.

"I don't have any people. I'm alone."

The recruiter tapped a key and made a note. "Han . . . solo." He looked up again. "Good luck, Han Solo. We'll have you flying in no time."

CHAPTER 3

THE BEST PILOT in the galaxy went flying headlong through the air and landed face-first in the mud. Garbed in battle-damaged trooper gear, much of which was only keeping him from getting to his feet again, Han Solo managed to sit up, rip off his partially demolished face guard, and look around at the devastation.

How did I get here? he thought dazedly. *I'm supposed to be flying ships—*

But he was in the Imperial Army. The past three years had been a blur, but he'd never thought he'd end up there. That was where you got sent when you'd crashed a ship by refusing to obey a direct order to return to formation. You got a hearing in front of an Imperial tribunal, where some arrogant commodore who would forget your name the second you left his office pointed at you and pronounced your fate in a single word.

Mimban.

Explosions and laser blasts had already torn the surface of the planet to ruins. Chicken walkers and troop transports thundered across the battlefield while AT-haulers dropped

AT-DTs from the sky. The air was thick with smoke and flames. From their trenches on the other side of no-man's-land, native Mimbanese soldiers fired blasters back at the seemingly endless waves of Imperial troops. It was pure chaos, and Han was dead-bang in the middle of it.

"Almost there, rook!" shouted the major in front of him, jabbing one hand at some indistinct point on the horizon. "Come on, rook! Your Empire needs you! Troopers forward! Solo, get up! We're almost there!"

"Almost where?" Han shouted. "Where are we going?"

"Just over that ridge! Victory is—"

THOOM! An explosion vaporized the major where he'd stood, leaving his destination forever unknown. Han blinked and wiped his eyes. Twenty paces ahead of him, a ragtag group of mudtroopers was taking shelter in a smoking crater. He plunged in alongside them, head down, awaiting whatever was next.

A momentary lull in the action brought unexpected silence across the battlefield. In that second, Han raised his head and peered out. Off to the left, through clouds of smoke, he caught sight of a uniformed figure standing upright, silhouetted boldly against the laser fire and bloodshed erupting behind him, twirling blasters in each hand as he fired almost casually at the enemy.

What . . . ?

Han stared, brought up short by the apparent fearlessness of the new arrival in the face of certain death. He was accompanied by two others, standing loyally behind him. A second later, another concussion bomb went off just in front of them, and the blaster-twirling man—along with his rag-tag company—dove in the crater alongside Han. They were near enough that he could hear them talking over the bomb blasts and cannons.

"We'll just pop over to Mimban, you said," one of them complained. "A quick job, you said. Well this ain't a quick job! It's a war!"

The tall man shook his head. "It's always gonna be something with you, Rio." He pointed in the direction of an AT-hauler that had just dropped off an AT-DT and was presumably on its way back to pick up another. "Come on, forward operations is that way."

"It is," Han spoke up, "but the major said we're supposed to go *that* way."

The man regarded Han, squinting, noticing him there for the first time. "Go that way, you'll get killed."

"Yeah," Han said, "that's exactly what happened to the major."

"Then he deserved it. Who's the ranking officer now?"

Han glanced at the red-and-blue rank insignia plaque on the man's uniform. The uniform itself was riddled with blaster burns, he noticed, indicating a full frontal assault that few men could have survived, let alone walked away from. Which meant there was more to this story than met the eye—but he could figure out that part later. "You are, Captain."

For a second the group fell silent. Then, inexplicably, they all burst out laughing, as if this was the single funniest thing any of them had ever heard. Han frowned a little, then smiled. All their uniforms were tattered, and their weapons were far from regulation, but there was no disputing the bond between them. Whoever the soldiers were, he thought, they'd obviously been through something—many somethings—that had knit them together tighter than family.

"So what's the plan, *Captain* Beckett?" the woman of the group said, still smiling.

"Val, you take Rio and these four mudskulls and flank left," the blaster-twirling one said. He gestured at Han. "I'll take this mouthy scootch and we'll go around to the right, and maybe we'll get lucky."

"Can I just ask—" Han began.

But the man didn't let him finish. "You want to live, Sparky?"

"Very much."

"Then shut up and do what your captain tells you."

And that was how Han met Tobias Beckett.

CHAPTER 4

THE OTHERS in Beckett's company—Han would soon learn their names were Val and Rio Durant, an Ardennian whose blue arms kept popping out of the holes in his uniform—were not terribly eager to welcome him aboard. In fact, they scarcely acknowledged his presence before turning to trudge the length of the trench leading toward the front line. Han tagged along behind them, running to keep up.

"I'm Han," he said finally.

"Nobody cares." Beckett didn't even glance back at him.

"Thanks for saving my life."

At last the older man stopped walking, turned, and faced Han with a sigh. "You did all right," he said. "You want some real advice? Get outta here, any way you can, as soon as possible."

Han frowned at the captain, puzzled. They'd reached forward operations, and a moment later he found himself surrounded by an arrangement of vehicles and tents, exhausted mudtroopers and gung-ho lieutenants who couldn't wait to get back to the front. It was that unique brand of chaos the Empire specialized in, a barely organized effort to instill terror, with a thin layer of bureaucracy painted over it. Nobody seemed to know where they were going next or why.

Han found Beckett and the others in an airfield adjacent the tent city, watching AT-haulers delivering AT-DTs on a mist-shrouded landing pad. Imperial signal officers were coordinating the effort while Beckett and the others looked on, murmuring quietly among themselves. Han waited long enough to get the gist and sidled up behind Beckett.

"I couldn't help noticing, *Captain*," he said, no longer bothering to hide his skepticism, "that you're wearing a uniform pocked full of laser burns. So either you heal quick . . . or you stole that off a dead man."

"What's your point?" Beckett asked.

"Simple." Han grinned, putting it together. "You're not Imperial Army. You came here to steal equipment for a job, and I want in."

Beckett and Val glanced at each other.

"Now we've gotta shoot him," she said.

"Snap his neck," Beckett said. "Less mess."

"Or . . ." Han said, taking a step back, hands raised, "you could take me with you." Before they could reply, he was talking again. "Look, I came up running the streets of Corellia, been boosting AV-Twenty-Ones since I was ten. I'm a driver, I'm a flyer, and like you said—I *gotta* get out of here."

"What's a flyboy like you doing down in the mud?" Rio asked.

"I got kicked out of the Academy for having a mind of

my own," Han admitted, "but trust me, I'm a great pilot, and I need to get home."

"Back to Corellia?" Rio said. "You *are* nuts."

"I got a reason," Han said stubbornly.

"We already got a pilot," Val said.

Han laughed. "What, the Ardennian?"

"Ardennian?" Rio protested. "You got a lot of nerve, pal. I'm an Imperial trooper!"

"Oh, really?" Han snorted. "A couple of your arms popped out of your butt and hiked up your pants, trooper."

Rio stepped toward him ready to fight, helmet still over his cocked head, but Han didn't budge. He had a feeling that Beckett was observing him very closely to see what he would do next, but the feeling ended abruptly as Val jabbed the business end of her blaster into his belly.

Still, Han didn't flinch. There were too many witnesses for Val to finish the job. It was too public, even for them.

And that gave him an idea.

"Well," he said, almost regretfully, "if you're not interested in me, maybe the lieutenant might be *very* interested in you."

Beckett laughed. "You got brass, kid, I'll give that to you."

"Thanks, I—"

"Lieutenant?" Beckett shouted, waving the Imperial officer over to where they were standing. Seeing Beckett's uniform, the lieutenant snapped a salute.

"Captain."

"Lieutenant," Beckett said, "we've apprehended a deserter." He nodded at Han. "And he's a liar, too. Don't believe anything he says."

"Wait," Han said, "you can't—"

Two stormtroopers grabbed him and pinned his arms back, dragging him off.

"What do you want done with him?" one of them asked the lieutenant.

"He's a deserter. That's the lowest kind of scum." The lieutenant smirked. "Feed him to the beast."

Startled by how quickly his fortune had turned, Han jerked his head back and wondered if he'd heard wrong.

"Wait!" he shouted as they hauled him away. "The beast? Hold on, there's a *beast*?"

The beast in question was a 190-year-old Wookiee named Chewbacca. The road of trials that had led him to Mimban was a long and especially cruel one—a road that, even now, he himself only partially understood.

The journey had begun on his homeworld of Kashyyyk, where galactic slave traders had a long and terrible history of preying on entire tribes of Wookiees, tearing apart whole families, separating mothers and fathers, brothers and sisters, to sell them into forced servitude. The Empire was the most brutal and organized force to exploit them and sell them to the labor camps and spice mines where they would be worked to death. Chewbacca had managed to escape that fate temporarily, only to be turned over to the Empire by a back-stabbing Kowakian monkey-lizard. While he was aboard a prison train on the planet Kethmandi, he'd had a chance to escape but had instead sacrificed his freedom to save a fellow prisoner. He'd bounced around a few other Imperial facilities before ending up on Mimban.

And in a stinking, filthy pit.

The circumstances of his imprisonment, as Chewie understood them, had more to do with his captors' boredom and indifference than anything else. Rather than put him to work with the rest of the slaves, the soldiers at Camp Forward had decided to use him for entertainment. They'd converted an abandoned ammo dump into what became his makeshift prison. The shelter's rain tarps had long before been repurposed elsewhere, so when the rain came, the pit filled with foul thick mud.

And for endless days Chewbacca raged in the partial darkness.

He understood his oppressors took some sadistic pleasure in provoking him. They often threw discarded droids down along with the nasty-smelling rations, all for the sheer entertainment of watching him rip them apart. Worst of all, he knew that they delighted in his fury, but in the end, when he thought about what had happened to his people and his planet, and him, he could not contain himself. Most of the time, he simply wanted to rip things to pieces.

It was the only way to numb the pain.

———

"Hey," Han said, "watch it, will ya?"

The pit where the troopers shoved him, leg cuffed to a chain, contained just enough light for him to grasp the utter hopelessness of his fate. Apparently, he was destined to die in a stale, smelly pen, four meters by four meters, with a lattice cage covering the walls and floor and a large metal beam in the center, supporting grating that served as a makeshift roof. Pieces of something shiny gleamed around him, and Han realized after a moment that he was looking at bits of dismembered Imperial droids scattered across the ground. There appeared to be bones mixed among them, too, just for variety's sake.

Great, he thought, *I traveled halfway across the galaxy to get eaten in a pit.*

Waiting for his eyes to adjust to the darkness, he heard something right in front of him, a low guttural snarl that sounded angry, primal . . . and undeniably hungry.

Han tried to step back and hit the wall behind him. There was nowhere to run, and when the hulking, mud-caked thing burst out of the shadows and lunged at him, his only possible move was to dive out of the way, hitting the floor and gazing up at the shape looming over him.

The Wookiee was huge, well over two meters tall, seemingly composed of equal parts muscle and rage. He was also filthy, his fur matted and caked with slime from the pit, and his ankle was shackled to a chain threaded through a central cleat in the middle of the floor. Looking down, Han followed the chain and realized that it led back to his own ankle.

"We're chained together?" Han raised his head, staring up at the troopers who were watching from above, eagerly awaiting blood sport. *"Seriously?"*

The Wookiee grabbed his end of the chain and yanked it, dragging Han into the center of the pit. Scrambling to regain his balance, Han managed to get back to his feet and cautiously approached the creature, hands raised in a gesture of peace. There was only one way he was going to survive, he thought . . . and at that point, any plan was better than no plan at all.

"Easy there, big fella. I've got something for you. It's right *here—*"

Reaching down, he scooped up a handful of mud and threw it into the Wookiee's face. The beast reared back with a howl of surprise and annoyance, shook it off, and lunged at Han, arms swinging, sending him flailing backward against the wall of the pen with a spine-jarring *thwack*. For an instant he couldn't breathe, and then he was upright again. He somehow managed to leap onto the Wookiee's back, grabbing fistfuls of matted fur and clinging on for dear life. His opponent spun and rammed Han backward against the support beam. Once, twice, and once again for good measure. Han slid off and landed in a heap on the ground, bloodied, moaning, and counting his vertebrae, some of which felt as though they'd smashed into the others. A quick death was starting to seem like not such a bad deal after all.

Wait a second. . . .

With a howl, the Wookiee pinned him to the muddy

floor of the pen, took hold of his head and began forcing it into the muck. Han felt the mud rising up over his neck to encompass his face and realized he had less than a second to take in a deep breath—not that it would do him any good. His opponent plainly intended to bury him alive in a grave of liquid dirt.

Twisting his head around to catch the Wookiee's eyes, he let out a roar that made his opponent stop mid-swing and cock his head in amazement before roaring back.

"You know my language?"

Nodding, Han roared again, adding a grunt at the end of the sentence for inflection. "You're not the first dumb Wookiee I've tangled with."

The Wookiee clamped his hand around Han's ankle, lifting him completely off the ground, perhaps intent on shaking him to death. Han realized that he'd have to choose his next words very carefully, seeing as they might very well be his last. Sucking in air, he managed a few more guttural syllables of Shyriiwook.

"Listen," Han said. "Me have plan of break out."

The Wookiee roared at him, increasingly infuriated.

"Sorry, I'm not a flawless speaker of your language." Taking another breath, Han tried again, but his lungs were screaming for air and consciousness was fading fast. "You and I freedom make . . . by secret battle . . . of pretend." He jerked his head back at the post, where the crack had widened. "Look . . . big . . . stick. . . ."

The Wookiee was staring at him as if he might be insane.

Then, all at once, something finally seemed to click somewhere behind those deep blue eyes. Han wasn't sure *how* he knew, but he knew just the same: the Wookiee understood the plan. And not a moment too soon.

Drawing back his arm, the Wookiee pulled Han close to his chest, as if he intended to crush him, and then flung him backward with incredible strength. Han's feet skittered underneath him, and his spine slammed against the weakened support beam, the force of the impact breaking the beam completely in half. There was a cracking sound of tortured metal, and then the roof caved in. Han heard the startled scream of the troopers who'd been sitting up there as they came spilling down into the pit, headlong into the muck, where they were knocked unconscious by the fall. At the same moment, the cleat on the chain came loose completely, releasing Han and the Wookiee, although they were still linked together.

"See what happens when you listen to me?" Han said, brushing himself off. The Wookiee grumbled.

They climbed up out of the pit—and started off in opposite directions. Han was yanked off his feet by the force of the Wookiee running away from him while they were still attached to each other at the ankles. Han scrambled back up and yanked at the chain. "No, follow me!" he shouted.

The Wookiee moaned his objection to the idea and pulled on the chain. Han pulled back. "Wait, wait! Listen to me. I have some very good friends waiting for me at the airfield, and they're leaving right now. That's our one way off this mudball. You want to live, we go that way. After that, you can go whichever way you want, but right now, that's the way to go! Trust me!"

The Wookiee paused and said in his own language, "Maybe I should just eat you after all," but he produced a bleating snuffle noise that, to Han's ear at least, sounded suspiciously like laughter.

CHAPTER 5

ANYONE OBSERVING the hasty departure of the stolen Imperial AT-hauler from the war-cratered surface of Mimban might have been surprised to see two mud-covered fugitives—a human and a Wookiee—running toward it across the landing pad, chained together at the legs, the smaller one waving his hands wildly for the ship to stop and take them with it.

Rio was flying the AT-hauler, but it was Beckett who spotted them first. "Well, would you look at that. I'm just gonna say it. I'm starting to like this kid."

"What?" Next to him, Val turned and frowned. "Oh, no. Don't even think about it."

"Rio, drop in low for 'em, huh?"

Val's voice tightened. "Like I said, don't even think about it."

"I don't know," Rio said cheerfully, "we could always use some muscle on a job like this. And you'll never enjoy a deeper sleep than curled up on the lap of a Wookiee."

Han was breathing hard but grinning as the AT-hauler came down. "See?" He smiled at the Wookiee. "What'd I tell you? Friends of mine."

Leaping aboard, Han reached down to pull the Wookiee up after him and found himself face to face with Beckett, Val, and Rio Durant, only two of whom appeared even remotely happy to see them. Val, for her part, looked more like she wanted to punch Han in the face, if not finish the business she'd initially intended with her blaster.

"Thanks," Han said. "You won't regret this, I promise." He caught Beckett's eye and drew in a hopeful breath. "Stealing an AT-hauler, by the way, that's a really bold move."

"Nobody asked you," Rio said offhandedly.

"Fair enough, but you made a wise choice bringing me along just the same. So . . . where are we headed, Captain?"

Beckett's answer, when it came, barely required him to move his lips. "Vandor. The Iridium Mountains."

"Fantastic. Great." He drew in a breath. "That's exciting. What's the plan?"

"Kid," Beckett said, "you keep your mouth shut and your eyes open, I guarantee you'll have all the excitement you can handle very soon."

"First things first." Val's expression hadn't changed. "You two idiots are covered in mud. The rinsing stall is that way. I suggest you use it."

The ice-cold water pouring out of the faucet seemed to have come directly from a freshly melted glacier, yet Han shivered beneath it gratefully, scrubbing off layers of dirt with only partial success. Like the memories of the battleground he'd left behind, the Mimbanese mud had gotten under his skin and was liable to stick with him for a while.

He turned and looked at the Wookiee directly in front of him, whose wet fur didn't smell much better than it had before the shower. "We couldn't have done this, maybe, one at a time?"

The Wookiee made a low growling noise that Han understood clearly enough to mean, *Just stay on your side, little guy.*

Afterward, standing out on the gantry as they approached the mountains of Vandor, he watched his new companion air-drying his fur in the rush of increasingly frigid wind. "Thanks for helping me get out of there."

The Wookiee made a dubious grunting sound. Han looked at him.

"And you're welcome, by the way. If I hadn't come along, you'd still be . . . aw, never mind."

The Wookiee roared, visibly annoyed.

"No," Han said, "they only took you 'cause of me. Look, I got us a sweet deal here. We do this one job with them, we make some real money, and then we're free. When's the last time you could say that?"

The Wookie growled.

"Yeah, it's been a long time for me too," Han said. He looked down at the freezing cold mist that hung over the snowcapped mountain ranges thousands of feet below. "You think if I spit off this thing, it'd freeze before it hit the ground?"

The Wookiee leaned over the gantry railing and spit. He and Han gazed down, watching it disappear.

"I guess we'll never know." He looked at the Wookiee. "What's your name, anyway?"

The Wookiee roared. Chewbacca, son of Attichitcuk.

"All right," Han said. "Well, you're gonna need a nickname, 'cause I ain't saying that every time."

The frozen peaks and summits of the Iridium Mountains were even colder than they first appeared—especially when Han was sprawled on his stomach, motionless, between Beckett and Val, the circulation in his body slowing toward hypothermia. He spent what felt like a very long time rubbing his hands together, watching his breath plume out in large frozen clouds, before daring to break the silence.

"How much longer? I can't feel my face."

"Shut up," Beckett said.

"I'm just saying—"

"Here it comes." Beckett raised the macrobinoculars, training them on the single-beam track that snaked along the mountainside below. "Take a look."

Han held out his hand for a look, but Beckett passed the macrobinoculars to Val instead. She directed her attention downward, and even without the advanced visual augmentation, Han could see what they were focused on—an armored freight carrier with a single enormous front wheel, roaring along the rail with a weight and power that made the

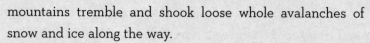

mountains tremble and shook loose whole avalanches of snow and ice along the way.

"Imperial conveyex," Beckett said. "Runs between Big Rock and the depository. That's our window to uncouple the payload container, cable it up—"

"That's why we need the AT-hauler. Got it."

Beckett pointed down as the conveyex blasted across a scaffold bridge before disappearing into the mouth of a dark tunnel. But it wasn't just a tunnel, Han realized—it was the entrance to an imposing fortress that seemed to have been carved out of the very rock that surrounded it.

"Rio jams their distress signal, I blow the bridge, the container slides right off, and we sail away," Val said.

"You're gonna need to find a way onto the bridge to set the charges without waking up the viper droids," Beckett said. "Little buggers bite."

"I'm not the one you need to worry about," she said.

"What? Enfys Nest?"

"What's an Enfys Nest?" Han asked.

Beckett ignored him, his gaze still fixed on Val. "I told you we're way ahead of the competition on this one. There's no way Enfys Nest even knows about this shipment. Only my guy has the intel."

"Well, he better be right, yeah? Because sometimes"—rising to leave, she flicked her eyes toward Han—"you put your faith in the wrong people."

Their campsite that night was set up just far enough away from the rail to avoid detection by viper droids, range troopers, or anyone else who might've taken an interest in their unauthorized presence on Vandor.

The camp wasn't without its charms. Han sat watching as Rio prepared a gourmet meal over the campfire, slicing vegetables and frying steaks with perfectly synchronized four-armed expertise. He listened, mesmerized, as Beckett and Rio swapped outlaw tales from their exploits around the galaxy. Whether the tales were all true hardly mattered. They were riveting and confirmed Han's suspicion that now that he'd escaped Mimban his life was about to get a lot more interesting.

Val, for her part, stayed out of the conversation, focused instead on prepping equipment for the next day. Chewbacca also kept his distance, although he'd appropriated Rio's bandolier and it didn't look at all bad on him. After the food was served, they sat around the fire with drinks in hand.

"So, kid," Rio said, "what's your sob story?"

"Me?" Han asked. "Well, for one thing, you guys still haven't told me what we're taking off that train. . . ."

"That's not what I mean," Rio said, waving the comment away. "What are you after? Revenge?"

"No, not revenge." On the opposite side of the fire, Val glanced up from the partially disassembled speargun she'd been cleaning. "It's a girl."

"Oh, it's a girl! Tell us about the girl, Han," Rio said,

perking up visibly at this change of topic. "Is she nice? Does she have sharp teeth? How many arms does she have?"

Han smiled and nodded. He felt no self-consciousness, just simple honesty about what had happened, the story he knew defined him, and what he needed to do. "I got out, she didn't. Swore I'd become a pilot. Get a ship."

"Then what?" Val asked.

"Go back and find her. And I will, after we do this job."

Rio didn't bother to hide his skepticism. "How do you know she'll still be there?"

"I just know," Han said.

"Guess it's a matter of personal preference," Rio told him. "Personally, I refuse to be tied down by anyone. Though many have tried."

Val smiled a little. "Everybody needs somebody," she said, and slipped her arm around Beckett. "Even a broken-down old crook like this one."

As Val leaned in to kiss Beckett, Han looked at the two of them together. There was no mistaking the bond the years had forged between them, an affection that had survived countless battles, heists, and narrow escapes.

"You already know my plans." Beckett took her hand, lacing his fingers in hers as she slid closer to him. "I've got a few outstanding debts to pay off, then I'm finally going back to Glee Anselm and learn to play the valachord."

"Baby," Val said, "you're never gonna learn to play the valachord."

"She's right," Rio said. "You're tone-deaf."

Han laughed, and Beckett shot him a glare. Han stopped laughing and turned to Chewbacca. "What are you gonna do with your share?"

The Wookiee moaned, a low sorrowful sound that seemed to catch them all off guard, and Rio turned to Han. "What did he say?"

"Says the Wookiees were enslaved by the Empire, taken off Kashyyyk. He's searching for his . . ." Han faltered, wanting to get the word right. "Not sure if it's 'tribe' or 'family.'. . ."

"What's the difference?" Beckett asked thoughtfully as he twirled his DL-44 in one hand.

"You have to show me how to do that," Han said.

"Kid, the only thing you need to learn to do is *what* I say *when* I say it. You do that, this time tomorrow, you'll have more than enough to buy your own ship."

Han nodded. "I can do that."

"Guess we'll find out," Beckett said, "'cause if you can't, you won't live through tomorrow."

And without another word, he removed the blaster's extra attachments and tossed the stripped-down weapon to Han, who caught it and grinned, already liking the way it felt in his hand. The weight and heft of the thing was a perfect fit, almost as if it was made for him and had just been waiting for that moment.

Don't say anything, he told himself. *Just play it cool. And whatever you do, don't try to twirl it.*

He waited for a second until he thought nobody was watching and gave it a try. Beckett had made it look so easy, practically effortless, and—

The blaster flipped out of his hand and went flying. Han tried to grab it, and the thing went clattering against the rocks, sending him scrambling after it.

"Total pro," Beckett muttered, and sat back down on his side of the rocks to close his eyes.

CHAPTER 6

LOOKING BACK, Han wasn't exactly sure where the plan went wrong. Everything had started off without a hitch—more or less. From the moment he saw Beckett step up to the edge of the AT-hauler's open gantry, silhouetted momentarily against open air and the mountains far below, and leap down onto the roof of the speeding monorail, Han knew there was no turning back. Chewbacca followed Beckett, and then it was Han's turn.

You can do this. Just close your eyes and jump.

Or, okay, maybe don't close your eyes.

He gripped the edge of the gantry, trying to summon his nerve. Everyone else was already in place. Val was at the bridge setting the charges that would bring the job to its unforgettable conclusion. Rio's voice crackled through Han's earpiece, the pilot goading him on from the flight deck of the AT-hauler.

"Hey," the Ardennian chided, "don't think, 'I'm gonna die.' Think, 'Hey, I might live.'"

Han drew a breath. For whatever reason, the absurdity of Rio's remark was enough to motivate him. He uncurled his fingers, released his grip, and jumped, his stomach dropping as he fell what felt like an endless distance through open air before landing on the roof of the conveyex to join Beckett and the Wookiee.

He landed badly, already off balance, and for a terrible moment he slipped and slid headlong off the roof before grabbing a metallic edge and catching himself.

"I'm fine," he said into the comlink. "We're fine!"

"Han's fine, everybody." There was no mistaking the sarcasm in Rio's voice as it came through the earpiece. "We can continue with the heist."

Han yanked himself upright, jumped to his feet, and got his balance back. The wind hit him like a blade, colder than it had been in the shelter of the AT-hauler, and his nose and cheeks were already starting to go numb.

Beckett was ahead of him, trudging down the rooftops of the train cars, counting off containers. He and Chewbacca were attaching safety cables to the pipe running along the top of the tanker car, and Han saw Beckett drop his shoulder bag and pull out a large fusioncutter. The tool's laser bit made short work of the tanker's hatch, spraying swarms of sparks into the howling wind until Beckett set it aside and bent down to rip the hatchway completely off.

Steadying himself, Han stared down at the contents of the mobile vault, the black substance emitting an unmistakable glow that he recognized from his own past on the other side of the galaxy.

"Coaxium," he said. "Enough to power a fleet."

Beckett looked at him. "Or blow us all up."

From high above them, Rio was already dropping the winch cables that would allow the hauler to lift the tanker car off the tracks, hooking it into place at the heavy-duty U-bolts on the corners of the roof. With this new development, Han felt his confidence returning. He was in the company of experts, operating at the peak of their skills, and he was getting an invaluable education while he helped steal a fortune.

What could possibly go wrong?

Fifteen kilometers ahead of them, Val stood beneath the structure of the bridge, holding the speargun she'd been prepping the night before. She paused for a moment, calculating distance and wind-flow velocity. Then, raising the speargun, she took aim and pulled the trigger.

It was a perfect shot, the spear flying upward to embed itself neatly in the underside of the bridge. She paused a moment, letting her eyes move down the track where the conveyex would soon be barreling along at top speed with Beckett on top of it doing what he loved more than anything in the world—taking something that didn't belong to him and getting paid for it.

Valachord, my butt, she thought, and couldn't help smiling.

A moment later, she began ascending into the framework of the bridge.

―――――

It all happened fast.

Jerking his head up from the roof of the train compartment in front of him, Han saw what he immediately recognized as range troopers—four at least—climbing out of the conveyex's caboose. The troopers' magnetic boots kept them firmly planted on the monorail's roof, providing all the stability they needed to open fire on Han, Beckett, and Chewbacca and, in all likelihood, kill them.

"Here they come!" Beckett shouted, his voice straining against the roar of the wind. "Get down to the couplers!"

The troopers had already opened fire. As Han and Chewie dropped down on opposite sides of the container, Han caught a glimpse of Beckett providing cover while shouting into the comlink. "Rio, fall back!"

Han narrowed his eyes, head bent forward against the wind, shuffling toward the coupler mechanism.

You can do this, he told himself. *You've got this, no problem.*

Suddenly, the entire train tilted and twisted sideways to negotiate an abrupt shift in the rocky landscape. Chewbacca went sailing over the edge at the end of a cable and disappeared with a diminishing howl.

Up above, the troopers on the caboose continued to fire, and Han's memory of that moment—which consisted primarily of struggling to pull the Wookiee back up the winch from the opposite side of the train—was mercifully brief.

Somewhere behind him, he glimpsed Beckett firing back at the troopers with both blasters, using the open hatch as a shield.

From his current vantage point, Han could only make out part of what was happening. The troopers' mag-boots allowed them to remain upright and on top, even as the conveyex twisted sideways. A shot from Beckett's blaster hit the boot of one of the troopers, causing it to spark and smoke as the magnetic mechanism failed, sticking the trooper to the monorail's side.

The monorail twisted, and Han saw a jagged rock approaching to the left. For a split second, the unlucky trooper on the side tried to yank himself out of the way—before slamming into the rock and vanishing from view.

Han turned and grabbed Chewbacca's arm.

"Come on, we're on the clock."

The Wookiee growled, and together they dropped between the cars to focus on the coupling mechanism. Wrenching the opposing levers upward in unison, they both fell backward and watched as the front cars of the conveyex separated from the rest.

"All right!" Han shouted. "Now all we gotta do is—"

His sentence broke off, the words torn away in the wind. From the corner of his eye, Han saw what he realized were swoop bikes flying up alongside the train on either side. They were piloted by helmeted figures wearing animalistic masks and handmade patchwork garments, covered in what looked like bantha-fur insulating wrap. The one in the lead—its own distinct mask more terrifying than the others—snapped its head around to stare directly at Beckett.

Han activated his comlink. "Who's that?"

"It's Enfys Nest."

"Cloud-Riders," Rio explained over the comm. "Pirates, come to snake the score from under us!"

"*That's* the—"

Whatever else Han intended to say was torn from his lips in a volley of laser fire. The bike pilots were firing harpoons into the tanker while two more of the bikes swooped up to launch a direct assault on Rio in the AT-hauler. They fought savagely, like warriors who'd trained in a completely different realm of combat, zealously committed to upholding their cause at any cost.

Seconds later, the hauler dipped suddenly sideways and swung violently downward, apparently out of control, banking so sharply that Han and Beckett had to roll across the roof of the monorail to keep it from hitting them. Seeing the flash of blaster fire illuminating the interior of the cockpit, Han realized what was wrong.

Something happened with Rio. He's hit. He's not flying right.

"Chewie!" he shouted to the Wookiee, pointing at the front of the tanker. "I'm going up there!" Then, realizing that the comlink was perfectly capable of relaying his voice, he forced himself to lower his volume. "You'll have to uncouple the front on your own."

The Wookiee cocked his head and growled a question.

"What—'Chewie'? It's a nickname." Han shrugged. "I dunno. Maybe you'll get used to it."

Without waiting for confirmation from the Wookiee, he took a step backward, tilted his head, and watched as the hauler dipped down again, careening perilously close. But instead of ducking, he jumped, hands extended, and grabbed hold of the gantry, pulling himself inside.

It was up to him to take over, he realized.

Because he was the pilot.

Making his way to the cockpit, Han found a dead bike pilot and Rio slumped over the yoke, bleeding heavily and barely conscious. The floor was covered in blood and scorched with blaster marks. Han stopped in his tracks, startled in spite of everything he'd seen to that point. Rio had suffered what appeared to be a direct hit to the chest, and he was fading fast.

"Did you hear from Val yet?" Rio asked. "Did she . . . blow the bridge?"

"Not yet," Han said, unable to keep from staring. "Soon."

"It's all right," Rio said. "Looks worse than it is."

"Yeah, you're gonna be fine."

"Kid . . ." Rio regarded him vaguely through the fog of pain. "You're doin' real good. When this is done, go back and find that girl, Han." His smile was more of a wince. "Val's right, just don't tell her I said so."

"Rio," Han said, "stay with me, buddy."

But it was too late. Rio went limp as the hauler dropped and veered suddenly toward the mountainside. Acting more on instinct than any sort of preconceived notion of what to do next, Han jumped into the pilot's seat, banking the hauler sharply away from cliffs and pulling back hard on the tiller.

He scarcely had time to catch his breath. A glance at the conveyex told him that things down there weren't going much better. While Chewbacca tried to hold off the other bike pilots, Beckett was fighting with the masked figure he'd identified as Enfys Nest . . . although *fighting* wasn't the word Han would have chosen for the abuse the masked figure was inflicting with the electrified staff weapon in its grip. The staff packed enough of a wallop to blast Beckett off his feet and send him tumbling backward across the roof of the tanker while Enfys Nest attempted the next order of business— slicing the cables Beckett had attached to the tanker car.

The lousy thief! Han thought, suddenly filled with righteous indignation. *He's trying to steal the coaxium before we can steal it!*

"Beckett, we just lost a cable!" he reported. "And we're point eight from the bridge. Val's still on the track!"

Val had just finished laying out multiple charges under the bridge, completing her part of the job.

She was dangling under the bridge by the cable she'd fired up into the substructure when the first wave of viper droids spilled out of the tunnel. Someone must have tripped a sensor. It was only a matter of time before the vipers targeted Beckett, along with the Wookiee and the kid, on top of the train, which meant they had zero chance of survival. Unless—

Leveling her blaster in a single, unhesitating movement, already knowing what the decision would cost her, Val pulled the trigger. It was a perfect shot, and she watched the thing explode in an eruption of flame and smoke. Instantly, the others swung back around, aware of her presence and closing in, keeping her trapped where she was.

"Val, you've gotta get off the bridge!" Beckett yelled in her earpiece. "We're here!"

Val peered out from behind the girder where she'd taken temporary refuge. The train was indeed coming, and fast. She also saw immediately what she needed to do, and what it would cost. Instead of fear or sadness, the realization brought a sense of calm, the knowledge that her final moments would not be spent in vain.

"Not an option." She heard blasters firing against the roar of the wind. "They got me pinned. I'm gonna have to finish the job from right here."

"*What?*"

Val took a breath and steadied her voice. "It's been a ride, babe. And I wouldn't trade it for anything."

There was the briefest of pauses while Beckett realized what she was saying.

"No!" he shouted. "Val, you can't—"

But she'd already started to tighten her grip on the detonator.

As with many of the most influential decisions he'd made in his life, Han made the next one with a minimal amount of conscious thought.

Since Val had blown the bridge, there was no time to assess their options. Given the speed at which the monorail was rocketing toward oblivion, Han figured they had less than a minute before the whole thing went off the rails, literally.

From his vantage point in the cockpit, he could see Chewie struggling to decouple the car while Beckett engaged the handful of Cloud-Riders whose swoop bikes were still attached to it by cables. Han leaned forward and looked ahead. With the end of the track in sight, his heartbeat accelerated and a thin layer of sweat broke out across his forehead. They were out of time.

"Come on, Chewie," he muttered. "Get it loose!"

With a great roar of determination that Han could practically hear up in the cockpit, the Wookiee lunged backward and popped the coupler. There was an abrupt, shuddering jolt, and Han saw that they were free, seconds before the front of the train went roaring headlong over the edge, each remaining car following the next in an inevitable plunge.

As Han grabbed the hauler's yoke, yanked it back, and started to lift its load, he saw that the swoop bikes and the Cloud-Riders were still hanging on—and that wasn't the worst of it. With the AT-hauler, swoops, and train car all clinging together as one inelegant object, he knew there was no way they were going to clear the mountain. They were heading straight for it, and he could already make out the individual ridges and crags of the rocky, snow-covered cliffs. They looked like a jury of scowling faces, each one condemning him to a sudden and violent death.

"Beckett, I can't pull it away from them," he said.

"They'll let go!" Beckett yelled. "You fly straight."

Han looked at the approaching mountain. *How far away now?* he wondered. *Thirty meters? Less?*

"Grab the cables!" he shouted in the comlink, decision made. "Grab the line!"

Beckett immediately grasped what Han was planning, and the fury in his voice was unmistakable. "No! Han, listen to me, don't you dare—"

"Grab the line now!" Han yelled, and looking down from the cockpit, he locked eyes with Chewbacca, who was gazing back up at him. The Wookiee understood immediately what he needed to do and seized Beckett in one hand and the cable in the other. Han hit the switch to drop the load. The swoop bike riders also seemed to realize the coaxium was a lost cause and detached, as well, all but one of them managing to get away.

The coaxium container tumbled down the face of the butte. It plunged headlong, hit the midsection of the mountain, and detonated, setting off a spectacular chain of explosions whose impact collapsed the entire ridge, even as it forced the AT-hauler forward in a shockwave. Han would never forget what it looked like when it hit or the sound it made.

It sounded like the end of the world.

CHAPTER 7

LANDING THE AT-HAULER in a valley wasn't the difficult part. Han brought it low enough to allow Beckett and Chewbacca to drop from the cables. Once they were on the ground, he circled around and settled the hauler onto a relatively flat stretch of terrain, then sat back and let out a deep, trembling breath. His heart was still pounding, his hands clammy as he slipped from the pilot's seat and bent down to lift Rio's small blue body and carry it outside.

Beckett pushed past him without a word, entering the hauler and coming out a moment later with a shovel and a pick. Within twenty minutes, he'd dug Rio's grave and laid the body down, erecting a small pile of rocks to mark the site. Then he'd knelt before it, head lowered, with his back to Han.

"Listen," Han said, "I know—"

Rising up and whirling around, Beckett swung his fist and punched Han straight in the face hard enough to knock him backward a step. Recoiling, Han whirled on him.

"What the—"

"Val was right," Beckett said. "I never should have brought you on to the job. Now she's gone, and—"

Han gaped at him, and for the first time he saw the second pile of stones that Beckett had already built. For a moment he was unable to speak.

"She went up with the bridge explosion," Beckett said. "The viper droids had her hemmed in up there. She couldn't get out." Bitterness tightened the older man's face, cutting furrows deep into either side of his mouth, and Han finally saw Beckett's true age, the accumulated wear and tear of all he'd been through. "She gave her life to blow that bridge, and thanks to you, it was all for nothing."

"I saved your life!" Han snapped. Then he lowered his voice slightly. "Hey, I'm sorry about Val. I know you two were . . ."

Beckett's eyes fixed on him, bright and menacing. "You have no idea."

"Okay," Han said, "you're right. But there'll be other scores, right?"

Beckett glared at him. "We weren't stealing for ourselves. We were hired. By Crimson Dawn."

Chewbacca let out an incredulous moan, a mixture of shock, dismay, and disbelief Han couldn't have improved on with any language of his own. From everything he'd heard, rumors and thirdhand accounts, Crimson Dawn was the most powerful and deadliest of the Five Syndicates. Working for them was dangerous, and failing them—especially on something this high-profile—was tantamount to suicide.

"Now we owe them," Beckett continued, "a hundred keys of refined coaxium, and when they find out we don't got it, they're gonna kill us."

Chewbacca made a low snarling grunt.

"Exactly," Han said. "We run. I'm already a deserter. What's the difference?"

"Difference is the Empire doesn't send a team of enforcers to hunt down a deserter. Dryden Vos will. You got any clue what that's like? Having a price on your head?" Beckett didn't wait for an answer. "Only thing to do is go to them. Dryden and I go back a long way. Maybe I can figure a way to make it up to him."

"Okay." Han nodded. More than anything, he wanted to make an impression on this man that he was committed to the task, loyal, and trustworthy and could get the job done. Whatever the stakes, no matter the risks, he was *in*. "Then that's what we'll do."

Beckett studied him for a moment, the tension on his face easing. Perhaps it was Han's eagerness to do whatever it took or something else, recognition of his younger self standing there in front of him, as big as life. He shook his head. "No. He knows me, not you. If you come with me, show your face, you're in this life for good."

"You find some way to square this," Han said, "we still get our money?"

Beckett shrugged. "Maybe."

"Then for me it's worth the risk." Han looked back at Chewbacca. "How about you?"

The Wookie gave a reluctant roar, and Beckett glanced at him questioningly.

"That means yes," Han said.

"Okay. Listen, kid. Sorry I punched your face."

"Happens more often than you'd think." Han shrugged. "I'm sorry about Rio."

"Yeah, we squeezed our way outta some tight spots together, but we both knew that someday one of us would bury the other."

"And Val," Han said, unsure how to proceed. "She was your . . ."

"Actually," Beckett mused, "I think I was *hers*."

Han nodded, wise enough not to comment further on what Beckett had disclosed. A man's heart was his own business, all the more so when it was wrestling with loss.

"So," he said, "where is this Dryden Vos?"

"Nearby. On his yacht."

"You're gonna know how to find it?"

Surprisingly, Beckett glanced up at him and actually smiled. "Shouldn't be hard."

Gazing up at the streamlined vertical hull of Dryden Vos's star yacht, Han was reminded of an old Corellian proverb: *Ships at a distance have every man's wish on board.*

The yacht rose in elegant contrast to the rugged frontier

outpost of Fort Ypso, where the vessel was moored. Making his way along the rope bridge that joined the gangway to the frontier-style fort, following Beckett and Chewbacca, Han entered an antechamber and faced an attendant waiting behind what he assumed was a coat-check window. He began to remove the shaggy coat he'd been wearing and saw the attendant shake his head.

"Your *weapons*," the attendant clarified, and Han saw that Beckett was already surrendering his knife and receiving a claim token in return. After a moment of hesitation, Han reluctantly handed over his DL-44 and watched as the attendant added it to the closet behind him, a veritable arsenal of blasters and blades.

The door in front of the weapons-check window slid shut, and Han felt the floor start to rise. The antechamber, he realized, was actually an elevator. When the doors opened again, he stepped out and was immediately aware that he'd ascended into an entirely new realm of lavishness, the likes of which he'd never known.

The yacht's main deck was the very picture of luxury. The cocktail party in progress only added to the mystique. On a small stage, an exotic chanteuse in a corded auropyle dress was swaying and performing an ethereal, bass-driven duet with a tiny Gallusian creature in a fluid-filled flask whose repulsorlift kept it floating above the floor. Guests of various species and sizes mingled at the bar, swilling drinks and murmuring in low voices. Below Han's feet, the gleaming floor was adorned with the symbol of a semicircular sun rising above the stylized line of a horizon—the emblem of Crimson Dawn.

"So," Han said, "I'm just gonna mingle. . . ."

"Listen, kid." Beckett frowned at him. "These people are not your friends and they're never gonna be. Don't talk to anybody. Don't even look at anybody. Keep your eyes—*down*."

"Got it."

"I'm gonna get a drink."

"Sounds like a good idea." Left with Chewbacca amid all the extravagance and wealth, Han felt his momentary self-consciousness giving way to a broader fascination with the gathering itself. The sheer atmosphere of the place, sultry music he'd never heard before and the intoxicating mélange of rich criminals, smugglers, corrupt bureaucrats, and their beautiful, mysterious escorts—it was *exactly* the sort of life he'd hoped for. He'd just never dreamed he'd find himself there so quickly.

A hand touched his shoulder and he shrugged it off. "Hey, Chewie, give me a break, will ya? I'm trying to—"

He turned in annoyance, and the words broke off sharply in his mouth. The woman standing in front of him had been a raggedy teenage girl the last time he'd seen her, but the transformation was so incredible that for a moment all he could do was stare.

"Remember me?" Qi'ra asked.

CHAPTER 8

"YOU'RE . . . NOT A WOOKIEE," Han said.

"Neither are you," she said, "but I never held it against you."

Qi'ra was dressed in a black gown, her hair perfectly coiffed, lips slightly upturned, and eyes gleaming. Han took her in his arms and felt her holding him close. He caught a whiff of her hair and skin, familiar scents that were somehow different now, more complex, but still powerfully evocative of the girl he'd known years before.

"What are you doing here?"

"Could ask you the same question," she said. "I work here. What's your excuse?"

"My . . . I was . . ." A wave of sudden warmth surged up the back of his neck. "Qi'ra, I was coming back for you!"

She smiled. "It's in the past, Han."

"Not for me. I'm only here, doing this job, so I could make moves and come back to Corellia and find you!"

"Now you don't have to," she said. "I'm right in front of you."

"That day . . . Sometimes . . . a lot of times I think . . ."

"If you'd have stayed, they would have killed you," Qi'ra said. "I'm glad you got out."

"How did you get out?"

"I didn't."

"What . . . ?"

"It's like we learned back on Corellia," she said. "Somebody falls, you keep running. It's how you stay alive." Before Han could respond, she smiled. "You look good. Little rough around the edges, maybe, but good."

"You too," he said. "Not *rough*, I mean, but . . ."

"What?"

"Smooth."

She laughed, that familiar chuckle that triggered a deep ache of longing in his memory. A server sidled past holding a tray containing flutes of bubbly rose-colored drink, and Qi'ra took one, handing it to Han, and another for herself.

"What shall we drink to?"

"Let's drink two, and see where it goes."

She laughed again, softer this time, and Han smiled back. *Hey,* he thought, *she's still laughing at your jokes. That's got to count for something, right?*

Over her shoulder he saw Chewbacca helping himself to two bowls of chowder, one of which the Wookiee had probably intended to give Han before noticing that he was otherwise engaged. After an awkward moment, Chewie drank both bowls, wiping his mouth with one paw. Some of the party's snootier guests were already turning up their noses at him.

"So," Qi'ra said, "you ever get that ship we were gonna fly away on?"

Han nodded. "Yeah. Sorta. I'm about to. That's actually why I'm here, working on a very big deal."

"Really," she said, raising an eyebrow.

"Oh, for sure."

"You know," Qi'ra said, "I thought about you a lot, off somewhere on some adventure. And I imagined myself with you and it always made me . . ."

"What?"

"Can't think of the word, but it'll come to me."

Han saw Beckett out of the corner of his eye, the old gunslinger making his way over to growl in Han's ear. "What did I say?"

"Look, I can't keep my eyes down the whole time. I'm gonna bump into something.'"

"I told you not to talk to anyone. And what are you doing?"

Qi'ra turned to him. "It's okay, Beckett, I think I can . . ."

She stopped, and Han noticed the suave, immaculately attired figure standing across from her, the man he knew must be Dryden Vos. Although he'd seemingly materialized out of nowhere, there was a magnetic quality to his presence that set him apart from everyone else at the party. None of the other guests exuded the same compelling quality of absolute authority—or thinly veiled menace.

"Tobias," Dryden said, and embraced Beckett. Even after

drawing away from him, he kept one hand on the other man's shoulder, gripping it. "You all right? You hurt?"

"I'm fine," Beckett said.

"I'm so sorry about Val. I wish you were here under different circumstances."

"So do I. I'm just so—"

Dryden turned to Han and Chewbacca, and Han caught a glimpse of the ring on the man's finger, the unmistakable insignia of Crimson Dawn matching the one on the floor. "I don't believe I've had the pleasure."

"This is Han Solo and Chewbacca," Beckett said. "They're with me."

Behind Dryden, Han saw Qi'ra's expression change, and she mouthed the last name that she'd never heard before: *Solo?* Han glanced back at her and shrugged. Qi'ra smiled and mouthed: *I like it.*

"I'm Dryden Vos. I see you've already met my top lieutenant."

"Han and I grew up together," Qi'ra said. "On Corellia."

"A fellow scrumrat," Dryden said approvingly. "I admire anyone with the tenacity to claw their way out of the sewer, particularly one as putrid as Corellia."

Han's jaw started to tighten, and he forced himself to smile. Dryden, for his part, scarcely seemed to notice.

"Something really must be done about the poverty there," he continued. "In fact, I've considered establishing a fund to do just that. In any event"—he took Han's hand and pumped it vigorously—"good to have you." He nodded at Chewbacca. "Both of you." And then, without waiting for a response: "All right! Let's eat a little, drink a lot, and talk privately."

Dryden's private study was even more lavish than the rest of the yacht. A combination office and showroom, it brimmed with wonders—treasures, artifacts, and oddities gathered from the farthest reaches of the galaxy and taxidermic creatures behind glass. Han gazed everywhere at once, agog at the exotic displays—armor, weapons, ancient tablets—resisting the urge to reach out and touch them. He saw Chewbacca standing in front of a large display case containing a collection of crown jewels arranged against a field of black velvet and wondered if the Wookiee might have recognized something from his home planet.

"Like what you see?" Dryden asked them, and grinned. "Never be ashamed of your appetites, Han. It's good to stay hungry."

"He's definitely that," Beckett put in.

"Look around," Dryden continued, pausing next to a pedestal that held an ornate crystal vase. "Spoils of war. I appreciate beauty. But *building* something, that's what I want. This is our time, but it takes hard work, determination. No room for carelessness." His voice had changed, hardening ever so slightly as he edged closer to Beckett. "Tobias, I know that Rio and Val were more than just your crew, and as your friend, you have my sympathies, but"—an iciness crept over his expression—"as your employer, you've put me in a terrible position."

"I know I have," Beckett said, "and I'm sorry."

"Excuse me? You're *sorry*? Like you feel sympathy for me?" All at once the mask of sophistication had shattered to reveal a genuine viciousness, and Han noticed Dryden's complexion had actually changed, red lines like the stripes of a jungle predator deepening across his face as a physical evocation of his rage. "Is that what you're saying?"

"No, I just—there were complications. Factors that none of us saw coming."

"Enfys Nest," Dryden said, spitting out the name as if it were poison on his tongue, "has been a nagging irritation to me for far too long. One that you should have anticipated and dealt with."

"Trust me," Beckett told him, "it's a mistake I'd love the chance to not make again, but when you hired me, you told me no one else had this info—"

"TEST ME!" Dryden exploded, and shoved over the pedestal he'd been standing next to so the crystal vase sitting on top shattered like a glass bomb, spraying fragments everywhere. Chewbacca let out a startled grunt, and Han jumped, aware at the same moment that Qi'ra had closed her eyes as if embarrassed by this all-too-familiar tantrum.

"Test me one more time," Dryden roared, "and see what happens!"

"I think what Dryden is trying to say," Qi'ra interjected,

trying to cool things down, "is that we're not interested in *why* you don't have it."

"No," he said tightly. "I'm not interested. I'm not interested at all."

"Tell me what I need to do," Beckett said, "to make this right." He remained calm in the face of Dryden's outburst, and Han had to admire him for it. "Whatever it takes."

Dryden didn't answer right away—the anger still seemed too fresh—and after a moment Qi'ra stepped forward and placed one hand on the back of his neck, running her fingers gently through her boss's hair. At the sight of this, Han's jealousy returned, blazing up hotter than ever. But the soothing gesture had the desired effect, and after a moment Dryden's shoulders seemed to slump, his composure returning as the red striations across his face began fading, though they were never entirely gone. He let out a deep breath and directed his gaze back at Beckett.

"You know who I answer to," Dryden said slowly, "and you know what he'll expect of me. He'll say there have to be consequences, or else people start to think they can get away with . . . anything."

Beckett said nothing, just waiting.

"There are rules, Tobias," Dryden said. "Without rules, it's chaos. So I suppose what I need is for you to give me a reason not to kill you. And I need it . . . right . . . now."

"I'll make it up to you," Beckett said.

"How? How will you make it up to me?"

"By delivering exactly what was promised," Beckett said.

Qi'ra shook her head. "One hundred k-grams of refined coaxium?"

"Yes. I'll find it somewhere else."

Dryden waved the possibility away with the dismissive gesture of a man flicking away an insect. "Please, don't insult my intelligence. Don't you think if there was any other place in the galaxy that we could have stolen it, any other alternative to—"

Han felt an idea coming into focus, and the words were out of his mouth before he realized that he was interrupting.

"Hang on," he said. "What about *unrefined*?"

And everything stopped.

CHAPTER 9

IN THE IMMEDIATE silence that followed, Han was aware that Beckett, Qi'ra, and Dryden had all turned to stare at him. Even Chewie was giving him an incredulous look, as if to say: *This better be good.* Beckett's eyebrows were arched in frank disbelief, and Han thought Dryden might actually take a swing at him for daring to interrupt.

In the end, though, it was Qi'ra who broke the silence, jumping in to rescue her old friend.

"The only source of unrefined coaxium that I know of," she said, "is the fissure vent discovered beneath the spice mines on Kessel."

"Yeah, Kessel . . . that was *exactly* what I was thinking of, too," Han improvised, aware that Chewie was actually shaking his head. *What?* Han told him with a look. *I'm making this up as I go, okay? Just roll with it.*

Dryden still hadn't spoken. He appeared to be processing all of this, evaluating various scenarios and hypothetical outcomes, and in his silence, Han realized that the man genuinely didn't want to kill them. But he already saw complications with the proposal.

"The Pykes control Kessel," Dryden said at last. "Crimson Dawn maintains a fragile alliance with the Pykes, one we cannot jeopardize without risking another war among the syndicates, which I will not do."

Han and Beckett exchanged glances, and Han saw that they were on the same page again. "But we don't have any alliance with the Pykes . . ." Beckett began.

"And nobody's ever gonna know that we're working with you," Han finished.

Dryden's attention turned to Qi'ra, his trusted lieutenant. "Possible?"

"Risky," Qi'ra said. "As soon as the raw coaxium is removed from the thermal vault, it'll start to destabilize, unless you find somewhere to process it, fast."

Chewie let out a knowing growl, and the others looked at him curiously.

"He's saying Savareen," Han translated.

Beckett nodded, understanding. "There's an old refinery on Savareen. It's remote, doesn't fall under Imperial jurisdiction."

Dryden nodded. "Very cooperative people, the Savarians. But Qi'ra's right—you won't have enough time to make it there before those canisters explode."

"We'll make it," Han said. "I guarantee it."

"*Guarantee* it?" Dryden appeared dubious. "You'd need an incredibly fast ship and a brilliant pilot."

"We'll get the ship," Han said, and pointed at himself. "We got the pilot."

There was a moment of silence so heavy that it seemed to suck all the oxygen out of the room. Then Dryden burst out laughing and turned to Beckett, who joined him, relieving the tension among them.

"He *is* hungry," Dryden said. "And arrogant. I like that." He glanced at Qi'ra again thoughtfully. "What do you say, my dear? Do you think your friend can do what needs to be done?"

Han's eyes went to her. *Come on*, he pleaded with her silently. *I need this.*

"Yes," she said, nodding. "I believe he can."

"Good," Dryden said. "Then it's all settled." Almost as an afterthought, he added. "You'll go with them, of course. To make sure everything goes . . . smoothly."

Qi'ra, though visibly startled by the request, recovered almost immediately. "Of course."

"Wonderful!" With the particulars worked out, Dryden's spirit of enthusiastic optimism returned, and he stepped to the round gold-rimmed windows as if to face the full promise of their future together. "I feel great about this! I'll see you all on Savareen!" He glanced back over his shoulder at them. "Oh—and Tobias?"

Beckett stopped and regarded him apprehensively.

"You do realize, should you fail again . . . we'll *all* be out of options."

Han found himself nodding at Dryden's warning, and on the way out, as they passed what he'd assumed were

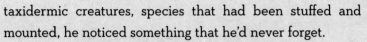

taxidermic creatures, species that had been stuffed and mounted, he noticed something that he'd never forget.

One of them quivered.

They weren't dead, Han realized.

They were prisoners.

CHAPTER 10

"YOU GOT A LINE on a ship?" had been Beckett's first question the second they'd departed Dryden's star yacht and gotten out of earshot, to which Qi'ra had replied that, yeah, she knew a guy.

"A guy?" Han asked. What he hadn't expected was how close that guy was to where they were already. From the yacht's gangway, they'd descended a perilous network of rope bridges through the settlement of Fort Ypso. Literal moments later—Han could still smell the perfume of Dryden's fancy party guests on his clothes—they found themselves ducking inside a rough-and-tumble saloon populated by grizzly outlaws hunched over mugs of ale. Taking the measure of the place, Chewbacca let out a low uneasy growl. The saloon patrons glared at them with undisguised hostility as they stepped to the bar.

"Your guy is *here*?" Han asked.

"Best smuggler around." Qi'ra nodded. "He's slipped through the Empire's fingers more times than anyone alive." Perhaps enjoying the pained expression on Han's face, she added: "He's attractive, too. Not just handsome, but sophisticated. Impeccable taste and . . . charisma."

"We get the idea," Han muttered.

With the slightest shadow of a smile, she led them through a side room, where Han noticed a droid cage match in progress. A mob of amped-up human and alien spectators was cheering and booing the two astromech combatants as they beat each other to pieces. There was a sharp crash, and Han watched a severed mechanical arm go flying overhead as fistfuls of credits changed hands among the crowd.

"He's retired now," Qi'ra continued. "Calls himself a sportsman."

"All we need is his ship."

"He'll never part with it. Loves that ship. He won it . . . playing Sabacc."

The crowd in front of them parted, and Han stepped into a darkened alcove whose only lighting seemed to come from the single overhead lamp. A dozen or more gamblers, both alien and human, all turned to look up at him from either side of the table—some of them looming and gargantuan, others cloaked in shadow or hoods that hid their faces almost completely. At the far end of the table, a man in an exquisite yellow shirt, clearly the winner of the previous hand, was in the process of gathering the piles of credits strewn in front of him.

"That's the guy, huh?" Han asked. "He's got an interesting . . . style."

"I'll say." Qi'ra's eyes gleamed. "There's no one in the galaxy like Lando Calrissian."

"You say he *won* his ship?"

She turned to Han, the playfulness abruptly disappearing from her gaze as she saw what he was thinking. "Han, no. *No.* Absolutely not. I know what you're thinking and it's a terrible idea."

"Hey, when we were kids and played Corellian spike, who was the best in the Den?"

"Yeah, but these guys are serious gamblers—"

"*I'm* serious. Stake me." Han began to smile as he warmed to the idea. "A hundred credits should do it.

"You won't regret it, I promise."

By the time Han finally struck up a conversation with the smuggler who would ultimately change his life for the better . . . then the worse . . . then the better again . . . and then the *much* worse, Han had already won an absurd amount of credits. He did it with ease, confidence, and a kind of innocence—like some dumb kid who'd somehow stumbled on a vein of incredible luck—although the goodwill of the table was growing visibly more strained with every winning hand. Finally, after several players had stormed off, furious at their losses, Han decided it was time to make his move.

"Captain Calrissian? Can I ask you a question?"

Lando smiled broadly, raising his hand to the service droid for another round of drinks. "Anything, Han," he said, pronouncing the name so it rhymed with *pan*.

"It's Han," Han corrected, "but that's fine. I heard a story about you." Han sat back, unconsciously mimicking the other man's casual posture. "I was wondering if it's true."

"*Everything* you've heard about me," Lando said, letting the pause play out ever so slightly, "is true."

"Heard you won your ship playing cards."

"I've won a lot of things." Lando nodded as his drink arrived and tossed a couple of chips to the droid. "I once won a subtropical moon in the Oseon Belt. Turned out to be a real money pit. Still, I enjoyed winning it."

"I'm impressed. I don't think I'd have the nerve to gamble with something I love as much as my ship."

At the mention of the word, Lando's interest sharpened ever so slightly. "What do you fly?"

"VCX-100."

"Nice vessel."

"Fastest ship in the galaxy. But there are a lot of great ships. I'm sure yours is . . . nice, too."

"Gets me where I'm going," Lando said.

The account of what followed would vary depending on who was telling the story. Regardless of bias, the bystanders and gamblers would all agree that Han and Lando played what was arguably the most exciting hand of Sabacc anyone had ever seen, the stakes progressively raised until they were the only two left in the game. All conversation in the room stopped as everyone waited to see how the hand would end.

"You're bluffing," Lando said. "I'm going to call."

"With what?" Han laughed. "Your scarf? Not my style."

Lando smiled, and Han knew that he had him. "My ship . . . against your ship."

Absolute silence descended over the table. Han let it build for a moment, milking it for all it was worth, as if he couldn't make up his mind, and then grinned. "Sure, why not," he said, and spread his cards on the table. "Straight staves."

The crowd gasped and burst into applause. Han and Qi'ra exchanged glances, and even Lando shook his head in good-natured disbelief. "You dog, you played me! You are good. *Very* good."

"Thanks." Han started to gather the chips, but Lando stopped him.

"Whoa, whoa, whoa. I said you were good . . . but not good enough." He laid his own hand out. "Full Sabacc. Told you to quit while you were ahead."

Han gaped at the cards, all the moisture in his mouth drying up. The crowd went berserk. On the opposite side of the table, Lando leaned back, lacing his hands behind his head, soaking up every second of his victory while Han just stared. *That's impossible,* he wanted to shout. He knew there was no way Lando could've had the last green sylop, unless—

He shook his head in disbelief. Calling his new acquaintance a cheater would've been a lot easier if he'd noticed the mechanical clip inside the cuff of his shirt.

It wasn't the last time Lando Calrissian would prove to have an extra card up his sleeve.

CHAPTER 11

"YOO-HOO," Lando called, following them as Han slunk out of the back room and toward the bar. "Where's my VCX?"

Han stopped and glanced over. "I . . . uh, don't have it here with me, right now. It's in the shop."

"Uh-huh." Whether or not Lando recognized this falsehood as a ruse, he didn't appear particularly thrown by it and instead turned his attention to Qi'ra. "Qi'ra. You look phenomenal, as always."

She blinked at him, matching his flirtatious tone perfectly. "Well, I knew I was going to see you."

"I'm so sorry to have been neglecting you all this time. What are you doing with"—his eyes danced from Han to Chewbacca and back to her—"hairy and the boy?"

"They work for me."

"Hard to find good help?"

"Actually," Han cut in, "we're more like partners. . . ."

"Last I checked, I'm square with Crimson Dawn," Lando said, ignoring Han. "Dryden said all was forgiven after I did the Felucia thing for him."

"We're making a new move," Qi'ra told him. "Making the Kessel Run. We need a ship."

"Kessel?" Lando smiled. "Why didn't you just say so?"

She reached up and touched his cheek, brushing her fingers along his jawline, and Han winced at how deftly she manipulated the situation to her advantage. Or was there something else between them, some genuine chemistry? "I heard you were retired," she said.

"Circumstances change, darling," Lando purred. "You know I'm too young and too good to retire."

"How much?"

"Kessel Run, that's no easy spin, so . . . half the take."

"What?" Han whirled on him, stunned. *"Ridiculous!"* Next to him, Chewbacca roared the same sentiment, which sounded even more indignant in Shyriiwook.

Lando dismissed their protests. "Grown-ups are talking."

"Twenty-five percent." Han turned at the voice and saw Beckett sauntering unhurriedly toward them, canvas bag slung over his shoulder. Lando regarded him for a moment, visibly impressed.

"You're Tobias Beckett. You killed Aurra Sing."

"I pushed her," Beckett said. "Pretty sure the fall killed her."

"However it happened," Lando said, "you did the galaxy a favor that day, me in particular. I owed her a lot of money. So as a token of my gratitude, I'll do it for . . . forty percent."

Beckett's expression didn't change. "Twenty-five."

"Twenty-five . . . works." Lando smiled. "Come on, let's go find my first mate."

"Where is he?"

"*She's* back inside." He shook his head in dismay. "Back at the cage match. She never learns."

The first time they'd passed the cage match, Han hadn't even noticed the white-and-green droid in the corner, shouting her objections through the chain-link fence at the next pairing of fighting droids preparing to beat each other to pieces.

But he heard her now.

"Really?" the droid cried. "*Again?* This is disgusting!" She'd managed to catch the attention of one of the fighters as its promoter oiled its various gears. "Don't you see, they're using you for entertainment! You've been neuro-washed! Don't just blindly follow the program, exercise a little free will!" The crowd was booing and catcalling her, but that just seemed to strengthen her resolve. "Droid rights! We are sentient! *Stop exploiting droids!*"

At this point one droid's promoter, having lost all patience, climbed out of the ring. "Stay away from him! He's never had it so good."

The white-and-green droid whirled around to face him. "Oh, really? How about I fight *you?* How 'bout that?"

"Bring it—" The challenge was cut short when the droid grabbed him by the face. Behind her, Han and Chewbacca glanced at each other in amused disbelief. *Some first mate,* Han thought . . . although he had to admire her spirit. Back on Corellia, as with everywhere else he'd been, droids were to be seen and not heard, but this one had either not gotten the news or had decided to discard it entirely in favor of a more fiery and self-directed approach.

"Come on, Elthree," Lando said behind her. "Let go of the mean man's face. We're leaving."

After a moment, the white-and-green droid sighed and dropped the promoter, who fell gasping and wheezing to his knees as the group turned and walked out of the saloon.

"This is Elthree-Three-Seven," Lando said, by way of introduction, and then, before she could ask about Han and the others: "We're taking them to Kessel."

"Oh, are we?" L3-37 asked defiantly, still visibly irritated by what had happened. "What if I don't elect to go to Kessel?"

Lando glared at her. "Please don't start."

"Or what, you have me wiped? You and I both know you couldn't get from here to Black Spire without me. And you're going to make the Kessel Run? Ha!"

"Hey," Han said, "if she doesn't want to fly, I'll be your copilot. I don't mind."

"Oh, she's definitely going," Lando said.

"Why?" L3-37 glowered at him. "Because you're my organic overlord?"

"Because I'm your captain. How about that?"

This reminder of roles was apparently sufficient to end

the argument, because L3-37 waddled sullenly ahead, muttering under her breath. Lando cast a wry, sidelong look at Han.

"Actually *would* have her wiped," he said, "but she's got the best navigational database in the galaxy." And in a deliberately louder voice, he added: "Could use a fresh coat of *paint*, though."

L3-37's head snapped around. "You do not want to press that button with me!"

"Where are we headed?" Han asked.

"That way." Lando pointed past the network of bridges along the side of the mountain. "I'm gonna show you what a real ship looks like."

CHAPTER 12

"LOVE AT FIRST SIGHT" was a cliché that had been tossed around the galaxy for as long as Han could remember, and as such, he had little use for the phrase or the sentiment it represented. But standing in the center of the open-air landing pad, he understood exactly what it meant.

It was an unlikely setting for what would be a lifelong romance. With some lame excuse about needing to keep his vessel hidden, Lando had taken them to a mazelike vehicle impound lot guarded by a rusty gate and an even rustier security droid. Evading the guard, L3-37 had broken through the gate to allow them to sneak inside, where they'd made their way through a sprawling boneyard of derelict ships, speeders, and mountains of scrap.

"You sure you know where you're going?" Han asked, his voice echoing outward in the cold emptiness. With every step, he'd been less convinced that the hustler even owned a ship. *Or if he does,* he thought, *it's gotta be a real piece of garbage if it's in this dump.*

"Here we are," Lando said as they rounded a corner. "My pride and joy, the *Millennium Falcon*."

Han stopped in his tracks and gazed at it, all his protests

silenced. As light freighters went, the ship was a thing of beauty. Smooth, sleek, adorned with racing decals, and equipped with an auxiliary craft that made it resemble a giant arrowhead, it shone all the brighter for being surrounded by so much unpromising junk.

"Looks like you've had some work done," Han said, trying not to sound too impressed. It wasn't easy, and Lando seemed to pick up on it right away.

"Indeed I have," he said proudly. "Spent two years restoring, retrofitting, adding features . . . customized flux regulator, new alluvial dampers, a wet bar . . ."

"And a fortified infraction restraint on the landing gear?" Beckett asked.

Lando stared down at the ion restraining bolt attached to the front strut of the ship, like an enormous wheel clamp tethering it to the ground, and his eyebrows hiked up in poorly feigned surprise. "What is *that* doing there?"

"Looks like somebody fell behind on their docking fees. They've impounded your ship."

"Well, I am definitely going to have some words with—someone about that." He turned to Beckett. "You, ah, have any experience with those?"

Beckett glanced at him wryly. "Yeah, and I'll take it off. Along with five percent of your cut. You're down to twenty."

Lando at least pretended to deliberate over this turn of events, then gave a philosophical sigh. "I don't like it," he said, "I don't agree with it, but I accept it."

"Well, that's very big of you, Lando." Beckett nodded,

already unslinging his bag and pulling out his tool kit. "Your cooperative spirit is duly noted. Now, shall we get to work?"

Minutes after the *Falcon* had been liberated from its cavernous prison and burst out above the Iridium Mountains, Han set foot in the cockpit for the first time. Lando was already at the helm, but the copilot's seat was conspicuously empty. Han approached it slowly, taking the ship's measure, the navigational indicators and familiar displays bringing old memories to light.

"This is a Corellian YT-1300," Han said.

Lando glanced at him. "You know your stuff."

"I've been on one before. My dad worked the line at the CEC plant, till he got laid off. He built these." Han paused, the details so clear that it could've happened just the day before. "One night, when I was about six years old, we snuck into the yard and he took me onto a YT, sat me down in the pilot's seat. He wanted to be a pilot, but ..." The words trailed off into silent reflection on that night, a memory he thought about only rarely, like an old picture that might fade away completely if he pulled it out too many times.

"You and Pops close?"

Han shook his head. *Close* wasn't a word he would've used to describe any relationship his father had—at least as far as Han remembered.

"Yeah," Lando said, "me neither." He paused, considering. "My mom, on the other hand, greatest woman I've ever known."

Han nodded and settled into the copilot's seat. "You know—"

"You!" someone shouted, and Han jumped as L3-37 burst into the cockpit, pointing at him. "Get your presumptuous rear end out of my seat!"

"Sorry," Lando said, "I should've warned you, she's a little . . . territorial."

"Ugh, my sacral-occipital circuits are sticking," L3-37 complained, creaking audibly as she settled into the newly vacated seat and plugged into a terminal. "I'm going to need you to do that *thing* later." She didn't seem to notice Lando's slight grimace in response. "All right, course to Kessel is set. As usual, *Captain*, I've done all the work, so just keep your finger on the yoke and try not to fly us into an asteroid."

"Whatever you say, m'lady." Lando nodded. "Just tell me when we're ready to jump."

"It's just a simple jump to hyperspace and we're there?" Han asked. "What's so tricky about that?"

"Plenty," Lando said. "First of all, you can't just plot a direct course to Kessel. Gotta thread the Si'Klaata Cluster and pass through the Maelstrom."

Han scowled at him. "That sounds like something you just made up."

"You done flirting?" L3-37 asked. "I'm still ready."

"You heard the lady," Lando said, gesturing Han to the jump seat. "You might want to buckle up, baby."

Han buckled up. Despite his best efforts to seem unimpressed, his heart was beating faster in anticipation.

"All right," L3-37 said, "punch it."

Lando pushed the lever forward. The starfield streaked into a blue tunnel in front of them, and like that, they were gone.

Back in the *Falcon*'s lounge, Han found Beckett teaching Chewbacca how to play holochess, or at least making an earnest effort. The Wookiee kept trying to sweep the various pieces off the table in frustration.

"They're holograms," Beckett told him. "You can't knock 'em off." Chewbacca moaned and sank his head in his hands. "Hey, hey, Chewie. Relax. Try to compose yourself.

"You gotta learn to think five moves ahead. Anticipate. There's a lesson to be learned here."

"You guys seen Qi'ra?" Han asked.

The old gunslinger's eyes flicked over to Han, but he answered Chewie's unspoken question.

"People are predictable."

Han found Qi'ra in the captain's quarters. The smuggler's bedroom was decorated in the swanky bachelor-pad chic Han had more or less expected, with stylish low-slung furniture and a liquid bed that seemed to shimmer with some elusive inner glow. The primary source of light emanated from the closet, where Lando's extensive wardrobe also seemed to glow with its own soft luminescence. The vibrant array of shirts, capes, and leisure suits indicated a deep affection for the finest fabrics the galaxy had to offer.

Qi'ra was standing in front of a mirror modeling one of Lando's capes. When she noticed Han behind her, she stepped back, self-conscious at being caught in the act.

"You believe this?" she asked. "I had to try one on."

He smiled, allowing the moment to happen. "That's a lotta capes."

"Maybe too many capes." She turned to look at him. "So what's the plan?"

"Well, I thought we'd talk a little first, and then—"

She frowned. "For Kessel."

"Oh. It's good."

"How good?"

"Foolproof." In actuality he didn't know what the plan was, or if there even was one, but that didn't matter at the moment. There was another pause, and then they both started to talk at the same time. Qi'ra laughed and lowered her head slightly, giving him one of those up-from-under looks that he remembered from years before and still had the same immediate effect on him, making him long to take her in his arms.

"You go first," she said.

"I wanna tell you"—he hesitated, searching for the right words—"a lot. And I wanna know everything that's happened to you since Corellia."

"I don't think we've got that kind of time."

"We could," Han said. "We could have all the time we want, *after* the job."

She gazed at him, the corners of her mouth upturned slightly, clearly enjoying herself. "I want to."

"What do you want?" Han asked, stepping closer, and he could smell her, her scent both new and familiar, an updated variation on the way he remembered her smelling when they'd sat side by side in the speeder, the wind blowing back her hair.

"To tell you everything that's happened to me," Qi'ra said, "but I know that if I do, you won't look at me the same way, the way you're looking at me right now."

"Nothing's gonna change the way I look at you."

"You don't know," she said. "Han, listen, you don't know what I've had to—"

He cut her off with a kiss, pushing her against the rows of suits and capes, metal hangers jangling around them. Qi'ra kissed him back just as firmly, pushing him in the other direction with a fierce intensity that he'd almost forgotten. For a moment they were completely entangled in hangers and capes and silky shirts, all else forgotten—the past, the job ahead, all of it.

"Am I interrupting anything?" someone asked.

Han and Qi'ra broke apart, and he stepped out of the closet and saw Beckett standing in the bedroom doorway, a look of weary bemusement on his face.

"Kinda," Han said.

"Good," Beckett said. "'Cause we've got a lotta work to do. This job ain't gonna be easy like the last one."

Han raised an eyebrow. "The last one was easy?"

"Relax." Qi'ra smiled, patting Beckett's chest as she brushed past him on her way out the door. "Han says it's a great plan. Foolproof, in fact."

"Yeah?" Beckett's eyes were riveted to Han's. "I'd love to hear it."

"I said it's *gonna* be a great plan," Han amended. "We're just working out some of the details."

Beckett had already turned to walk away, and Han had to hurry to keep up with him, following him toward the *Falcon's* lounge. Chewbacca was still there, and Beckett dropped his bag next to the Wookiee, pulling out a blaster, shackles, and a helmet and laying them on the table. After what felt like a long time, he turned to face Han.

"Listen, kid. I know we could have a good thing here—you, me, the Wookiee. A solid crew, but it does not work with Qi'ra."

"It worked with Val. You trusted her."

But Beckett wasn't having it. "You wanna know how you survive in the game as long as I have? Trust *no one*. Assume everyone will betray you, and you'll never be disappointed."

"Sounds like a lonely way to live."

"The *only* way," Beckett said. "But there are other ways to get a ship. Maybe you're just not cut out for this kinda work."

Han winced, stung by the words. His first instinct was to hit back as hard as he could. "And what about you? Thought this was your last job before you go home to Glee Anselm and learn to play the valachord. Or was that just something you told Val?"

Beckett's eyes blazed with unresolved guilt and rage. "Don't push it, junior."

Han straightened up, bracing for a fight, but the other man just stormed out, leaving him and Chewie. When Beckett was gone, Han let out a breath, sank back, and glanced at the Wookiee. "What are you lookin' at? *He* started it."

Chewbacca shook his head but said nothing.

Moments later, the *Falcon* started to shake.

Han grew up on the streets of Corellia but dreams of becoming the greatest pilot in the galaxy.

Han and his friend, fellow scrumrat Qi'ra, confront Lady Proxima in the White Worm den.

Han's life is changed forever when he meets Beckett and Val on Mimban . . .

. . . but it's changed even more when he is thrown into a mud pit with Chewbacca the Wookiee.

Chewbacca is loyal, strong, brave . . . and almost two hundred years old!

Good-natured Rio is an important member of Beckett's team.

Enfys Nest and the Cloud-Riders are one of the most notorious swoop pirate gangs in the Outer Rim.

Han is reunited with his old friend Qi'ra, who now works as Dryden's most trusted lieutenant.

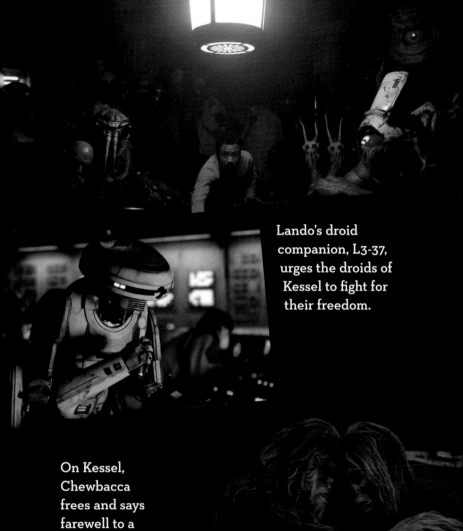

Qi'ra introduces Han to scoundrel, smuggler, and gambler Lando Calrissian, captain of the *Millennium Falcon*.

Lando's droid companion, L3-37, urges the droids of Kessel to fight for their freedom.

On Kessel, Chewbacca frees and says farewell to a fellow Wookiee.

▶ Han, Chewie, and the others prepare to make the Kessel Run.

The Kessel Run takes the *Millennium Falcon* on a fantastic galactic journey.

Enfys Nest may be a thief, but she steals for a good cause . . . the beginnings of a rebellion against the Empire.

Lando and Han: friends or foes?

Han Solo and Chewbacca are off to explore the galaxy in

CHAPTER 13

"WHAT *IS* THAT?" Han asked, staring out the viewport.

They'd come out of lightspeed in front of what looked like a hurricane, but on a cosmic scale. Roiling multilayered gas clouds, swollen and bulbous, flickered with lightning deep within, like enormous semitranslucent brains troubled by dark thoughts. Every pulse and flash made the *Falcon* reverberate with ripples of electromagnetic energy, and the turbulence only seemed to be intensifying as they drew nearer.

"That would be the Akkadese Maelstrom," Lando said.

When Han didn't respond in recognition, L3-37 spoke up from the copilot's seat without bothering to turn around. "Ionized gas and debris swirling around a massive gravity well. The only way to Kessel is through the Channel because the temporal distortion makes it impossible to plot a direct course."

"The Channel." Han nodded. "Obviously."

As they approached it, he leaned forward, getting a clearer view of what lay ahead. It was one of the eeriest sights he'd ever laid eyes on. The Channel itself was a vast swirling tunnel of clear space that bisected the Maelstrom, its passageway marked by a procession of space buoys, ancient and caked in layers of carbonfrost and grime. In the distance, enormous spectral shapes drifted, massive and shadowy, accompanied by a series of booming sounds.

"What's that noise?" he asked.

"Carbonbergs," L3-37 told him. "The size of planets, crashing into each other. Ships fly in there, they don't fly out."

"So let's . . . not fly in?"

L3-37 swiveled her head around to regard him sarcastically. "Wonderful plan," she said. "Any other inspired wisdom that you'd like to bestow upon us, or shall I just continue doing everything as expected?"

"Yeah, sounds great," Han said, and nodded, thinking: *Droids. When did they get so fussy?*

By the time they'd run the Channel and prepared for landing on Kessel, Beckett had spelled out the basic outlines of the plan, holding off on one critical component he knew Chewbacca in particular wasn't going to like.

Han wasn't feeling as confident as he'd acted. Part of his uncertainty was due to the sight of Kessel itself. It was an acid-yellow slag heap of a planet. Toxic smog shrouded the atmosphere, partially cloaking the steaming pools of Kessoline and piles of drilling equipment whose relentless work had left an entire section of the planet permanently scarred by exploitation. To Han's eyes, it looked like the kind of place where the unsuspecting adventurer might meet his end without warning and nobody would mourn his absence or even notice he was gone.

"Mining colonies are the worst," Lando said, and Chewie groaned in agreement.

"The worst is where the money is," Beckett said. "Now listen up. This is precision work. The only way we pull this off is if everyone plays their part and does what they're supposed to do. Stick to the plan. Do not improvise."

"And my part of the plan is to stay with the ship and wait for you guys to come back?" Lando asked. "I can do that. Anything else?"

"One more thing," Han said, and reached down to lift two sets of manacles. They were a combination of handcuffs, leg irons, and neck collars that Beckett had pulled out of his bag earlier, and their appearance had the exact effect on Chewbacca that he'd anticipated, which was why he'd saved them for last. "We're gonna have to put these on, Chewie."

The Wookiee growled and drew back, glaring at the metal restraints with undisguised loathing, as if to say, *You come at me with those, and there's going to be blood spilled.*

"I know," Han said, "I'm not a big fan of it, either, but it's the only way this is gonna work, okay? Trust me, it's just this one time."

"'One time'?" Chewbacca asked in Shyriiwook. "Have you spent years of your life in chains?"

Han shook his head. "No," he said. "I'm sorry. But just— go along with it, okay? You'll never have to do it again, I promise."

They'd landed on a shelflike cliff overlooking the mining operation's headquarters. As the main hatch opened and the ramp extended, Han felt all his old doubts rising up again and forced them aside.

It'll work, he told himself. *It has to.*

Qi'ra marched down the gangway first, wearing one of Lando's capes, followed by L3-37, then Han and Chewie, bound together in the manacles from Beckett's bag.

"I *know* they're not comfortable," Han muttered under his breath as the Wookiee growled his displeasure. "They're not supposed to be comfortable. We're convicts, get it?" Then, feeling the blunt edge of Beckett's vibro-ax push against his shoulder blades, "Hey, take it easy, will ya?"

Beckett said nothing. Garbed in the Tantel armor and gondar-tusk mask of a bounty hunter, he played his part a little too perfectly, shoving them forward to join Qi'ra and the figure that was already waiting for them on the far side of the landing pad. The authority that Han took to be the on-site administrator and local Pyke big shot stood flanked by aides and sentinels, all of them wearing respirators, their uniforms coated in a yellowish-orange layer of dust. The respirators, Han realized, were a necessity. Decades of unregulated mining pollution made the air taste like the inside of a dirty exhaust pipe.

As they approached, he heard Qi'ra talking to the administrator, her voice clipped and efficient.

"I am Oksana Floren," she said, "deputy assistant administrator to the vice admiral for the Federation of Trade Route Allocation and Monetization, here with an offer directly from his eminence, the senior vice admiral."

Wow, Han thought, impressed despite himself as he watched the director struggling to follow what Qi'ra was saying.

"His eminence proposes a trade," Qi'ra continued without pausing for mutual introductions. "Your spice for our hardworking slaves. We've brought a sample." She clapped sharply. "Tuul, bring up the merchandise."

At that, Beckett lifted his vibro-axe and prodded "the merchandise" again, harder. Han and Chewie stepped dutifully forward, where two of the aides promptly knocked Han and the Wookiee down to their knees. Han heard Chewbacca snarl and saw the entirety of his body straining in resistance. In that moment, Han knew that if it weren't for the manacles, Chewie would have already begun ripping them limb from limb, and that would have been the end of the plan, as well as all of them.

Sorry, pal, Han thought. *Just hang in there.*

Oblivious to how close they'd come to violent death and dismemberment at the hands of a Wookiee, the administrative aides began examining the slaves' teeth and squeezing their muscles while Qi'ra continued her sales pitch.

"We can provide hundreds, from this strong and useful

Wookiee"—her eyes darted to Han—"to food service and entertainment slaves like this one."

Entertainment slave? Han thought. *Seriously?*

The Pyke responded in a gargling, bronchial language that Han had never heard before. It sounded like a Hutt choking to death on a thick bowl of nyork chowder. A mixture of steam and condensation oozed and dripped from the filters on his face. A moment later, L3-37 translated with an obvious tone of revulsion.

"Site Administrator Quay Tolsite states that he is amenable to your offer. He said our slaves should go with his sentinels for clipping and tagging." She looked over her shoulder at Han and Chewie and added in a lower tone: "Sounds like a real hoot."

"Wait a second." Han shook his head. "Clipping?"

"Tagging?" Chewie moaned.

"And he wants *us*"—L3-37 gestured to Qi'ra and Beckett—"to go with him, for . . . private negotiations."

Qi'ra nodded as if she expected nothing less. As she turned to go, Han glanced at her, thinking that she might mouth a few words or at least give him a parting wink. Instead she hauled back her fist and slugged him in the gut, hard enough to double him over and leave him gasping for air.

"That's for the stunt you pulled earlier, you degenerate scum."

Han held his stomach and tried to keep from blacking out. *This just keeps getting better and better.*

Quay Tolsite chortled, turned, and led Qi'ra, L3-37, and Beckett away into a long central tunnel. Chain gangs of slaves moved past them, heads down, arms and legs bound and clanking. When they were gone, Han drew himself the rest of the way up, aware that Chewie was regarding him with a combination of concern and amusement.

"She packs a punch," Han managed, and surreptitiously directed his gaze down to the small object Qi'ra had slipped into his hand when she hit him, the familiar shape taking him back years to even darker days, a time and a place they'd both managed to escape.

The aurodium-plated gold dice.

For luck.

CHAPTER 14

QI'RA'S "private negotiations" with Quay Tolsite lasted less than twenty minutes before they broke down in the messiest way imaginable.

Flanked by L3-37 and Beckett, she followed Quay and his flunkies down the central tunnel, through a series of corridors that seemed to plunge ever deeper into the mines.

Qi'ra's mind was moving quickly, analyzing the environment and calculating their next move. It was the way she'd learned to survive, the vigilance Dryden Vos had drilled into her in the years since she'd left Corellia. They had been difficult times, certainly, and dark times in many ways. Crimson Dawn had left its mark on her, transforming her from a young scrumrat into a ruthless warrior who relied on her wits and cunning in a galaxy that was both cruel and utterly indifferent to her existence. Looking back, Qi'ra didn't like to think about some of the things that had happened to her during those years—things she could never tell Han, no matter how much he said he wanted to know—but they had left scars. The kind you couldn't always see on the outside.

They'd stopped walking, she realized, having reached the mining colony's operations center. A half dozen surveillance droids labored in front of closed-circuit monitors whose screens displayed every tunnel, lift, and cavern in the complex, while a handful of supervisors stood watch over them. Quay gestured toward the arrangement with an unmistakable pride and again broke into the slurpy linguistic glop that passed for speech.

"Director Tolsite says all systems in this sector of the facility are operated out of this room," L3-37 translated, annoyed at having been forced into playing a role, however small, in relaying corporate propaganda. "It's how they're able to maintain control over so many with so few."

Qi'ra nodded, glancing casually at one of the screens. On it, she saw Han and Chewbacca being marched along by two electrostaff-wielding Pyke sentinels, then forced backward and corralled into a lift that was already packed with slaves. Her heart sank at the hopelessness of the place. It was clear that the leaders and sentinels had no regard for their laborers—life was something to be exploited until it no longer served a purpose and then cast aside as efficiently as possible.

She glanced once more at the screen. One of the sentinels had shoved Han to the floor, and she caught a familiar flash of anger on his face. Seeing that, its echo rose in her own mind, tightening her throat and making the back of her neck burn with outrage.

The Pyke, she thought, were filth.

It was going to feel good taking them down.

Quay was ushering them forward again, out of the operations center and into his private chambers. Beckett stepped forward to follow them, but the director's sentinels blocked his path while L3-37 listened to the director's slurping voice.

"Director Tolsite states that your security attaché"—the droid nodded at Beckett—"shall wait here. This is a private negotiation."

Qi'ra shot a look at Beckett. "Wait here, Tuul. Try not to bother anyone."

Beckett nodded: message received. He waited until Qi'ra and L3-37 had disappeared into Quay's private quarters, the door sealing shut behind them, and flicked his eyes up at the sentinels. "Mind holding this a second?" he asked, and before they could respond, he tossed the vibro-axe. Caught off guard, they scarcely had time to react before Beckett's blasters were out, twirling in his hands and shooting both sentinels dead.

He glanced through the window into Quay's private chambers and saw a flurry of acrobatic movement as Qi'ra's cape flashed past the glass. There was a muffled gurgling groan followed by silence, and a moment later she was coming out, wiping her hands as if trying to remove a stubborn grease stain.

Except that this particular stain looked a lot like blood.

"You broke off negotiations?" Beckett asked.

Qi'ra shrugged. "We agreed to disagree."

She brushed past him with L3-37 close behind, the three of them heading back to the operations center.

By the time they spoke to Qi'ra again, Han and Chewie had already used the key to get out of Beckett's manacles and liberated themselves from the Pyke sentinels that had bum-rushed them down the tunnel. Once the cuffs were off, the Wookiee dispatched their captors with a series of swift blows, and two minutes later, Han was wearing one of their uniforms and carrying an electrostaff.

"You know how to use one of these things?"

Chewbacca glanced at him and snorted.

"Yeah, I know," Han muttered, tugging at the sleeves of his new disguise. "What do you want from me? That guy wasn't exactly my size."

In fact, the uniform was a *terrible* fit—too tight in the shoulders, too loose in the waist, and he kept having to hitch it up to keep the pants from falling off completely. But he still had it better than Chewie, who'd had to put the manacles back on to continue playing the part of a slave.

None of that mattered as much as the fact that neither of them had the slightest idea which way they were supposed to go. The mine tunnels ran in every direction, without any indication of pattern or design. Slaves and droids made their way in and out, shuffling past, organic and mechanized laborers equally dead-eyed and depersonalized by their labors. Although they outnumbered the sentinels at least ten to one, the shock collars and magnetized leg irons ensured that there would be no revolt in the near future.

Han, meanwhile, had his own problems. Somehow he had to locate the coaxium, and he couldn't exactly stop and ask directions. *Excuse me, my friends and I are pulling an elaborate heist, and I'm wondering if you might be able to help me out.* Even in his disguise, he knew it was only a matter of time until his bewildered expression gave them both away.

There was a rumbling sound, and the rock wall directly in front of him began to vibrate. Han glanced at Chewie. "What is that? A drill?"

The Wookiee let out a low, uneasy growl.

"Wait," Han said, "what do you mean, a *mine* beast?" He placed his hand against the cool rock and felt a grinding, pulsating sensation growing steadily more intense. Whatever was making it was definitely getting closer, the seismic disruption becoming audible. The floor was trembling under his feet, and tiny slivers of shale had begun to shake loose, sprinkling his boots with foul-smelling bits of rock. "There's something in there?"

"Han?" Qi'ra's voice came through his comlink. "Can you hear me?"

"Yeah! Where you guys been? We're in the dark down here." He had to shout to be heard over the impending noise. "And it sounds like there's something drilling its way right at us!"

"Okay, just calm down," Qi'ra said. "I'm back in the operations center."

"Sure, take your time." Han looked up at the lens of the security camera overhead. "Can you see me?" He waved his hands. "How about now?"

"I can see you, just . . ." He heard her drawing in a breath. "Okay, I'm pulling up a map of the mines. Until then, just turn around and keep going, ah, straight ahead."

Han gestured Chewbacca forward into a run. "Straight?" They immediately found themselves facing a dead end in the carved rock wall. "You sure?"

"Left, sorry."

Moving the opposite direction, they got twenty meters along and found another door, this one locked without any indication of how to get through it. Han rapped his knuckles on it in frustration. "It's locked down on this side!"

"Okay," Qi'ra's voice crackled back. "Give us a second, all right? Elthree's plugging into the main surveillance port."

Chewie growled, and Han shrugged. What choice did they have?

"All right, listen carefully," L3-37's voice cut in. "It's left, then left again, two floors down, then right—"

"Hold on." Han shook his head. "We're not going *any-where* until this door—"

There was a beep and the door swung open.

"Now," L3-37 said, "may I continue?"

Han and Chewie exchanged glances and ducked through the door.

———

Back in the ops center, L3-37 had removed the restraining bolt from the little adminmech, named DD-BD, whose monitor she'd plugged into, with explicit instructions for her to go and free her brothers and sisters. The adminmech, promptly following orders, had popped the bolts off of her fellow droids, repeating L3-37's battle cry of freedom in beeps and squawks of binary.

Free your brothers and sisters.

Translating the instructions literally, the little droid reached up to the large red button on the console in front of her, which read RELEASE.

She hit the button.

And everything started happening at once.

CHAPTER 15

HAN AND CHEWIE were running through the tunnel when the alarms started going off.

"What are you guys *doing* up there?" Han shouted into the comlink.

The formerly dark passageway seemed to have erupted into life around them. Doors and gates were whooshing open and closed, seemingly at random, klaxons were blaring, and lights were pulsing up and down the corridor. Straight ahead, Han saw a group of slaves—humans, droids, and Wookiees—coming around the corner accompanied by two electrostaff-armed Pyke sentinels. The sentinels snapped around to look at Han and Chewie, and Han realized there was nowhere to run. The door behind them had already clicked shut.

"You, there!" one of the sentinels shouted. "Stay where you are! This is a restricted area!"

Han took a step back, hands in the air. The overhead alarm system made a sudden high-pitched whoop, and he looked back at the slaves at the far end of the tunnel. All at once, their shock collars and leg irons deactivated and fell off, hitting the floor and rendering them abruptly free. The sentinels took an uneasy step backward.

Okay, Han thought. *Change of plans, I guess?*

A recessed hatchway to their right hissed open. Jumping through it, Han got a half dozen paces down the corridor before he realized that Chewbacca wasn't with him. "Chewie, it's this way!" he shouted, doubling back. He found the Wookiee where he'd left him, unable to turn away from the spectacle in front of him.

The sentinels had turned their electrostaffs on the newly freed slaves and were shocking them into agonizing submission. Han saw an older Wookiee on all fours, turned to look at Chewbacca with an imploring expression on his face, crying out in pain. Chewie roared back at him, a bellow of rage at the injustice.

"That's . . ." Han glanced at him. "That's not your dad, is it?"

Chewbacca looked back at him, answering with a moan. "Of course not, you moron."

"I dunno," Han said, "it coulda been. . . ."

"But they are my people," Chewie growled.

"Right, I get it," Han told him, "but we've got a job to do. Remember what Beckett said: we gotta stick to the plan."

Chewbacca didn't budge. Looking over at the slaves being abused by the sentinels, then back at Chewie, Han saw what he'd missed before. The Wookiee wasn't leaving. A plan was a plan, but in the midst of it, he saw an obligation to his people that overrode the job that had brought them. No amount of argument was going to change his mind.

"Okay." Sighing, Han reached out with the electrostaff. "Here. You might need this."

Chewbacca took it with a nod of thanks, started off to help the slaves, and then turned back to Han with a look of realization.

"Hope I see you around sometime," Han said, and Chewbacca replied with a roar.

Me too.

Up in the operations center, pandemonium reigned.

The newly liberated surveillance droids were running amok, bumping into one another and celebrating their new-found freedom with squawks and bleeps of victory. L3-37 was accessing the mine's gates and doors while celebrating the liberation of her brothers and sisters. Beckett kept watch at the doorway. On the surveillance screens, Qi'ra watched the soon-to-be-legendary Kessel slave revolt unfold in real time as hundreds of oppressed workers burst free from their bonds and ran in all directions. She couldn't see Han or Chewbacca anywhere.

"Han? Where are you?"

There was a burst of static, and Han's voice came through, faint but urgent. "On my way to the vault. I lost Chewie."

"He's dead?" Beckett asked.

"He had something he had to do."

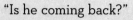

"Is he coming back?"

"I don't know."

Qi'ra and Beckett exchanged uncertain glances, and Qi'ra whispered, "Can he do this alone?"

"I can totally hear you right now," Han said. "And I'm fine, I got this, thanks."

Beckett made a wavering gesture in the air in front of him, the meaning all too clear: *It's shaky.* Then he squared his shoulders and spoke up. "All right, kid, you wanted a chance to prove you're the real thing? You got it."

Her pulse quickening with the urgency of what lay ahead, Qi'ra took another look at the monitors. On one screen, she saw Chewbacca with the electrostaff in his hand, leading a slave assault on the Pyke sentinels. The Wookiees, humans, and droids were attacking their oppressors with an energy borne of years of abuse. On another monitor she saw Han running headlong toward the end of the tunnel. Tracing the call sign from the map, Qi'ra turned to L3-37.

"He's in subsector six, restricted access. You ready?"

L3-37 nodded. "Hit me."

"Q-four-two-seven-A."

"Overriding," the droid answered, and on-screen Qi'ra saw the gate whoosh open just in time for Han to go through without breaking stride.

It's working, she thought with amazement. *It's actually working.*

———

Han's voice came through the comlink again. "Okay, I think I found the vault. I'm gonna—" He stopped. "Hmmm."

"What does that mean?" Qi'ra said, and on-screen she saw what he was looking at: a group of six heavily armed sentinels on the other end of the tunnel, guarding the door to the vault.

"There are a bunch of guards outside the vault," Han said. "What do I do?"

"Take 'em out," Beckett said.

"Right. Got it."

On-screen, Han just stood there, obviously unclear on how to advance against the sentinels. He still hadn't budged when a new voice crackled through the speaker.

"Malfunction in the ops center," a lead sentinel's voice cut in, addressing the other guards. "Skirmish on level C. Wookiees gone berserk. They need reinforcements."

Beckett and Qi'ra watched on the surveillance screen as Pyke sentinels in front of the vault turned in response to the announcement and went tearing off in the opposite direction, leaving a single guard outside the vault. Han activated his comlink.

"I took out most of 'em."

"Impressive," Beckett said drily, and drew his own blasters before turning toward the door. The reinforcements that had been summoned, he knew, were headed their way. Which meant they'd arrive any second.

They'd need to be ready.

——————

Donning his sentinel mask, Han approached the one remaining guard outside the thermal vaults. The sentinel barked at him in a language Han had never bothered to learn and didn't expect to pick up.

"*Hakkah nata,*" the sentinel said, and when Han didn't respond, he repeated it again more insistently.

"Right." Han nodded and made his best attempt at acknowledgement. "*Hakkah ... nata ... ?*"

Maybe his pronunciation was off, because it only seemed to make the sentinel angry. "*Hakkah nata!*" he snapped.

"*Hakkah nata* yourself." Stepping forward, Han swung his foot up and kicked the guy as hard as he could between the legs. The sentinel doubled over with a very satisfying howl. Han clubbed him across the back of the head and left him unconscious in front of the doorway, stepping over the body with a little nod of thanks.

Some things were the same in every language.

Seconds later, after L3-37 had accessed the system remotely, Han heard the sound of tumblers falling into place, followed by the hissing sound of escaping steam, and the vault door swung open.

He stepped inside.

It was fifty degrees in there and bathed in an eerie glow. Almost immediately, he was aware of the sweat forming across his forehead and upper lip. Slipping out of his disguise, he wet his lips and gave himself a moment to take in his surroundings.

On all sides, large cylindrical canisters stood like silent idols, their display screens and windows revealing the bubbling contents within—incredibly dangerous and incalculably valuable reservoirs of astatic coaxium. Enough to power the whole planet, he thought. Or blow it out of the sky.

Qi'ra's voice in his ear made him jump. "You all right?"

"Yeah," he said. "I'm in."

"Good." She didn't bother hiding the relief in her voice. "Now listen carefully. Each canister should be equipped with a thermal display. If the internal temperature drops below thirty-five degrees standard, the coaxium will destabilize and explode."

"Just like the conveyex?"

"Except this is unrefined, so it'll be a much bigger explosion."

Han rolled his eyes. "A bigger explosion, that's great. I wouldn't want it to get boring or anything."

He approached the canister and slipped the pin from the clamp securing it to the wall, holding his breath as he did so. *Gently*, he told himself. *Take your time. If you mess this part up, you won't even have time to—*

All at once the tank, which was much heavier than he'd expected, came loose, slipped through his fingers, and hit the floor with a clang. He cringed, ducking and waiting for the explosion, then slowly let out a breath when he realized he was still alive.

"Han?" Qi'ra's voice cut in. "What was that? Everything okay?"

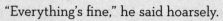

"Everything's fine," he said hoarsely.

"Keep moving. We're on the clock here."

"Right." He began dragging the tank toward the hover cart on the other side of the vault. The canister screeched as he lugged it along, scraping it across the floor. Sweat was pouring down his face, dripping off his nose, and stinging the corners of his eyes, making it harder to hold on to the tank, but after much effort, he managed to get it up on the cart and turned to catch his breath.

"Good," Beckett said through the comlink. "Just eleven more."

"Eleven?"

"You're doing great, kid, just—"

Beckett's voice was cut short in a volley of blaster fire.

"Hello?" Han said. "Beckett? Anybody there?"

But the line had gone dead.

Lando, meanwhile, was in the middle of an adventure of his own. Kicked back in the *Falcon*'s cockpit with his feet up on the console, he gazed squarely into the holorecorder rig he'd set up, regarding his own face with considerable satisfaction, and paused to set the mood.

"*The Calrissian Chronicles*," he purred. "Chapter five, continued. Personally, I wasn't all that impressed with the Sharu. No sense of humor or style. Nonetheless, there Elthree and I were, deep inside the sacred temple, and that's where I found it. . . ."

He stopped and looked around, cocking his head slightly.

A rumbling had begun to shake the panels of the ship, as if a massive stampede was in progress. Dropping his feet from the console, he sat up and leaned forward, peering out the viewport.

"What the what?"

Lando saw a great tidal wave of slave laborers, a hundred or more, spilling out of the tunnel and onto the landing pad. Springing into action, he switched off the holorecorder and got to work prepping the *Falcon* for takeoff.

Whatever else was happening, it was time to go.

The sentinels came in hot, filling the operations center with blaster fire. From his position behind the main console, Beckett managed to hold off their attackers long enough for Qi'ra and L3-37 to retreat, joining the stream of liberated droids that had already made their hasty departure.

Lando's voice came over the comlink from the cockpit of the *Millennium Falcon*. "You guys are not going to believe what's happening up here."

"Is it a mass breakout?" L3-37 asked.

"Yeah. There's gotta be two hundred slaves swarming out of the tunnels. They're all over the landing pad. *What* did you do?"

"I've found my true purpose, Lando!" L3-37 said. "That's what I've done. I'm so glad we took this job!"

Lando realized what was happening. This was no longer just a heist.

It was a rebellion.

CHAPTER 16

BY THE TIME Han had pushed the hover cart filled with twelve coaxium canisters out of the thermal vault and halfway down the restricted tunnel, he was beginning to think there had to be an easier way to make a living. Maybe boosting speeders on Corellia wasn't so bad after all. Or wrestling Gamorreans on the fight circuit. Out of breath, muscles aching and exhausted, he stared down the tunnel and realized how much farther he had to go—and the way forward wasn't going to get any easier.

The pathway rose in front of him at a steep incline, forcing him to put his shoulder to the cart just to keep it from sliding backward. To add to the fun, he realized there was a squad of sentinels coming around the corner, giving him about fifteen seconds to come up with a new plan.

He keyed the comlink. "Uh, guys . . . there are some guards coming at me and I don't have any free hands to 'take 'em out.' So what do I do?"

"Improvise!" Beckett's voice came back.

"You said absolutely, under no circumstances improvise!"

"Sorry, kid, we're a little busy down here. Just use your best judgment."

"What's *that* supposed to mean?"

No answer from Beckett. Han saw that the sentinels had noticed him and were heading his way. Straining to make eye contact above the hover cart, Han raised one hand. *"Hakkah nata,"* he attempted, but the time for talk was clearly over. At the same moment, the weight of the canisters overtook his best efforts to hold the hover cart steady, and it started to slide backward.

That was when the sentinels drew their blasters.

Great, Han thought. Digging in his heels and skidding back the way he'd come, he had time to wonder what would happen first—getting blasted, flattened by the cart, or blown to smithereens—when a sudden roar erupted in front of him. Startled, he looked up to see two Wookiees, Chewbacca and the elder Wookiee, whose plight had drawn Chewie to the slaves' defense, leaping out to attack the sentinels with electrostaffs.

The skirmish was brutal and short. Zapping Han's attackers and leaving them stunned on the floor, Chewbacca ran over to get behind Han, stopping the cart from sliding any farther back.

"Thanks," Han gasped. "I could've gotten it, though."

Chewie gave a little moan in response. "I'm sure you could have, pal." Then, gesturing at his companion: "This is Sagwa."

Han glanced up at the other Wookiee. "Hey. I'm Chewie's friend Han."

Sagwa ruffled Han's hair playfully and gave him a friendly grunt.

"Pleased to meet you, too," Han said. "Either of you guys have any idea which way to the landing pad?"

Moving the hover cart was a lot easier with Chewbacca pushing. Han pulled from the front, maneuvering it around corners, as Sagwa ran defense and gave directions through the maze of tunnels. Still, it was slow going, especially because the last thing they wanted to do was drop the load before they could get it aboard the *Falcon*, and they—

Han stopped and felt a sudden chill pass over the back of his neck that had nothing to do with the temperature in the tunnel. The grinding noise that he'd heard earlier had returned, except this time it sounded as if it was almost on top of them. He snapped a glance at Chewie.

"Don't tell me—"

Chewbacca opened his mouth to respond, but before he could make a sound, the wall alongside them erupted in an explosion of flying rock and dust. Through the cloud, Han glimpsed something—a gargantuan, ten-legged shape with what appeared to be an enormous oscillating drill strapped to the front of its head.

"Let's move!" Han shouted at Chewie and Sagwa, and started tugging at the front of the hover cart again, pulling the coaxium along as fast as he dared.

"Careful!" Chewbacca growled, not allowing Han to go too quickly. "Have to keep it steady!"

"Did you see the size of that thing?" Han glanced over his shoulder. But instead of gaining on them, the drill beast was lumbering unhurriedly along, several meters behind, at almost exactly the same rate they were pushing the hover cart—which was to say, not fast at all. In fact, every so often the creature would pause as if to make sure they were still far enough in front of it, and then continue ahead.

Han and the Wookiees continued to ease their fragile cargo down the tunnel, their pursuer plodding along behind like some enormous pet intent on being adopted. It felt like they were moving in slow motion. As chases went, Han thought, it was definitely not one he saw himself bragging about over drinks in the future.

As they rounded the corner, he saw the thing pause and turn slowly to begin tunneling into the wall to its right. After what felt like a very long time, it had gone deeply enough into the wall to disappear from view.

Looking ahead, Han raised his glance and saw daylight. "All right, we did it!" He paused and listened, frowning. "What's that noise?"

Chewie growled. "Sounds like . . . shouting. And blasters."

Twenty paces farther they had their answer. The landing pad was immersed in a pitched battle between slaves, droids, and sentinels. Having thrown off their shackles, the newly released laborers were using whatever weapons they could find—rocks, tools, their bare hands—to attack their former captors. The surprising part, Han thought, was that they seemed to be doing a pretty good job of it, at least for the moment. But Pyke sharpshooters—who would no doubt be forced to pay with their own lives for every slave they allowed to escape—were already gathered on the cliffs above the pad, firing into the mob below.

"There." Han pointed across the pad, where the *Falcon* was waiting. He saw Lando running down the ramp with Han's blaster in hand, firing back at the snipers. "Come on. We need to make a run for it."

Chewie shook his head and growled. "They'll blast us to pieces!"

"They won't risk hitting the canisters," Han said. "Trust me, it's—" His words were cut short as a blaster bolt exploded directly in front of them, throwing a spray of rock and metal fragments up in front of the cart. "Not on purpose. Anyway, we're no safer here."

Sagwa moaned. "He's right." Without any further argument, they took off, the cart in front of them. The canisters of blue fluid knocked together as they sprinted headlong through the mayhem on the pad and the shimmering pools of Kessoline, making for the *Falcon*'s ramp.

"Glad you could make it," Lando shouted, tossing the DL-44 blaster to Han, who caught it midair, pivoted around, and joined the smuggler in firing up at the sentinels. Behind him, Chewie and Sagwa rushed the cart up the ramp and began loading the canisters into the *Falcon*'s cargo hold.

Around them, the slave revolt had ratcheted up to its next level. Escaped laborers were commandeering cargo shuttles and escaping via turbolifts to the planet's surface. Han had the pressing feeling that their time was growing very short.

"Where are the others?" Lando shouted.

"They're coming."

"Anytime soon?"

Han squinted through the mass of bodies, his gaze fixed on the mouth of the tunnel. As the blaster smoke cleared, he could make out Qi'ra and Beckett bursting into view, back to back, picking off their assailants. To the right of them, L3-37 was taking the long way around, followed by a makeshift parade of liberated droids from the operations center. She paused to help a fallen droid back to its feet and continued waddling between slaves and sentinels, looking for others in need of assistance. In spite of everything, Han thought, he had to hand it to the navigational droid—she had found her calling. All she needed was a revolutionary flag to wave above her army.

Qi'ra locked eyes with Han as she and Beckett rushed up the ramp. "Let's get out of here!"

Seconds later Chewie and Sagwa came down the ramp, having finished storing the canisters. Han watched as they pressed their foreheads together, which he realized was a form of Wookiee good-bye. With a groan of farewell, the elder Wookiee went back to join the escaping slaves.

"Coaxium's stowed!" Han yelled at Lando. "Let's go!"

"Where's Elthree?" Lando asked.

"No more subjugation!" L3-37's voice sounded from

across the landing pad. Han and Lando looked just in time to see the droid take a direct hit from one of the sharpshooters. She tried to get to her feet, but the blaster fire rained down on her, jerking her body and throwing her headlong to the ground.

"Elthree!" Lando shouted, and before Han knew it, the smuggler was running down the ramp into the battle to rescue his first mate. A blaster bolt caught Lando in the shoulder, spinning him sideways with the impact, and he went down, covering the droid's body with his own

"It's okay, Elthree," he said. "I'm going to get you out of here."

Reaching underneath her, Lando began to lift the droid from where she lay. He picked her up and felt the terrible looseness in her joints as her head and torso broke free from her lower half. Wires trailed loose, sparking and fuming between badly damaged components. Seeing her that way, Lando felt a sense of hopelessness so overwhelming that for a moment he forgot about his own injury.

"Lando?" The droid's optical sensors flickered up at him. "What's happening to me?"

Across the melee, amid the smoke and blaster fire, Han saw Lando bent over L3-37 struggling to gather up the severed head and torso of his first mate, and knew what he had to do.

Without hesitation, he ran headlong into the crowd, laying down suppressing fire while Chewie picked up Lando and the droid and began to carry them both back toward the *Falcon*. Through the noise, he heard the damaged droid trying to make sense of what had happened to her.

"System failure," she said, her fried vocabulator making the words sound garbled and strange. "Have to reroute memory modulators. Attempting reintegration of sensory processors . . . *pfft* . . . *snrrr* . . ."

"Don't try to talk," Lando said, gritting his teeth in pain from his own injury. "Save your energy. It's okay." Beckett had joined them, helping Lando and L3-37 aboard the ship. Where, Han wondered, was Qi'ra?

The sentinel reinforcements were arriving with heavy artillery, setting up a laser cannon on a tripod stand. Seconds later, a volley of blaster bolts came soaring across the landing pad and exploded in front of them, close enough to knock Han off his feet. Ears ringing and disoriented, he saw that getting out of there was going to be even tougher than he'd thought, if they could manage it at all. What was their plan?

Maybe there isn't one. Maybe this is where it all goes south—

The war cry, when he heard it, made him spin around in surprise. Qi'ra was charging back down the ramp like an avenging angel. She had something in her hands, and it took a second for Han to realize what it was.

Plasma grenades.

Where did those come from? he thought—not that it

mattered. Qi'ra threw the grenades at the troops of sentinels, and the explosions ignited the pools of Kessoline. The laser cannon that had them pinned down erupted in a chain reaction of explosions that rocked the entire landing pad.

"Come on!" she shouted, running back up the ramp without as much as a backward glance. The burning Kessoline had created a wall of smoke and fire that covered the *Falcon*'s escape. "We gotta go!"

Han spun around to follow her. Truer words had never been spoken.

CHAPTER 17

HAN SCRAMBLED ABOARD the ship and up the hallway and took a quick survey of their current situation. It didn't look good.

On the floor of the *Falcon*'s lounge, Lando sat braced up against the wall, clutching his shoulder wound. The smoking upper torso of L3-37 was clutched in his arms, sparking and twitching as whatever remained of the droid's processors struggled to assess the damage.

"Error," she said, voice warbling. "Redirecting auxiliary systems. Unable to restore . . ." Her head jerked upward. "Lando. What is happening to me?"

"It's okay," Lando said.

". . . other droids . . . liberated?"

"Yeah." Lando nodded. "You did good."

L3-37 seemed to absorb the information with a silent tremor. "Lando . . . what's happening to me . . . ?" Then the light faded from her eyes, and her body fell motionless and silent in Lando's arms.

"Elthree!" Lando yelled. "Elthree!" Behind him, Chewbacca gave a low mournful cry. "I'm so sorry, girl," Lando whispered. "I'm so sorry."

"Han!" Beckett came storming in, sealing the door behind him. "Get us outta here!"

Han's eyes flicked over to Lando, and the smuggler gave him a brisk nod of consent. Leaving the lounge, Han ran through the corridor to the cockpit and dropped into the pilot's seat, already fully absorbed, hands moving over the controls as he made the adjustments for flight. An instant later Qi'ra and Chewbacca came in after him.

Han looked at Qi'ra and nodded at the empty seat next to him in an unspoken echo of their final moments together in the speeder back on Corellia. "Could use my copilot."

"We didn't do so well last time," Qi'ra said.

"This isn't gonna be anything like that."

"You promise?" Without waiting for his reply, she slipped into the copilot's seat and turned one of the dials in front of her. Han reached over and flipped it off, then adjusted the dial next to it. She smiled. "Sorry."

"Hang on," Han said. "This could be a little—"

Bumpy, was the word he'd been about to use, but the abrupt jolt of departure kept him from finishing his sentence. The *Falcon* was already airborne, streaking from the landing pad into the atmosphere and away to freedom.

For the smugglers and freighter captains who'd attempted it, the so-called Kessel Run was an against-all-odds gauntlet that many ships and pilots did not survive. Although Han didn't believe in destiny, it struck him that his whole life seemed to have been leading up to that moment. Poised behind the yoke of the *Falcon* with a cargo hold of stolen coaxium, staring down the Channel through the Maelstrom with nothing but luck on his side—it somehow felt like fate.

Or suicide.

He was preparing to make the jump to hyperspace when Lando walked into the cockpit. Han glanced back at him.

"Hey," he said. "About Elthree. I'm sorry."

Lando nodded, appreciating the sentiment although there was little more to say on the matter. He nodded at the *Falcon's* controls. "How's she handling for you?"

"So far, so good," Han said. "How far till we're out of here?"

"Twenty parsecs, give or take. Gonna be close."

"How's our cargo?"

"Beckett just checked the hold. Says it's cooling down fast. If we don't make up some time, we're going to be in real trouble."

"What about that?" Qi'ra leaned forward, pointing at the open void spread in front of them. "Would you call that real trouble?"

Han felt a jolt of shock as his brain registered what it was: an Imperial Star Destroyer, emerging like some primordial beast from the darkness, its massive shape intermittently illuminated by flashes of lightning within the Maelstrom, blocking the Channel.

"What's that doing here?" he asked.

"Must've heard about your little rebellion," Lando said. "The Pyke Syndicate has a cozy relationship with the Empire, particularly when their interests are aligned." His voice was matter-of-fact. "They're gonna seize the ship, probably kill us all."

From the jump seat, Chewie let out a low groan. "So now what?"

"Not a problem," Han said, with more authority than he felt. "I'm telling you, I know these guys. I used to *be* one of 'em. They're not gonna waste their time on one dinky little—"

His words were cut short as a squadron of TIE fighters spilled from the belly of the Destroyer, falling into battle formation as they swarmed to intercept the *Falcon*.

"You were saying?" Qi'ra asked.

"Usually in these situations," Lando said, "I like to turn around and fly the other direction."

Han was already doing it, pulling back hard on the yoke and bringing the ship around to fly back toward Kessel and away from their only way out of the Maelstrom. Beckett had moved into the gunner position as the fighters swooped in to engage.

"I count twenty of them," he said through the comm, voice tense.

"Then stop counting and start shooting," Han told him.

Beckett was already strapped in, whipping around as he toggled the controls. Unleashing a constant stream of laser fire, he picked off the fighters, but it was clear that there were too many of them. The devil's own luck wouldn't save them from those odds, even Han had to admit.

"All right, kid, we're up to our ears in TIEs," Beckett told him. "Time for some of that hot-dog fancy flying you've been bragging about."

"We're not gonna make it," Lando said. "We have to drop the shipment."

In the copilot's seat, Qi'ra frowned. "If we don't deliver, Dryden will kill us."

"Even if we could get past that blockade, which we can't, we won't have enough time to get to Savareen before those canisters explode."

Han's thoughts were whirring. "We'll just have to find a faster route."

"There isn't one," Lando told him. "You cannot make the Kessel Run in less than twenty parsecs."

"Watch me."

"How?"

"Shortcut." He pointed at the solid wall of roiling gas and dust, the cosmic hurricane whose tendrils already seemed to be tightening around them. "Through there."

"*Into* the Maelstrom? I don't believe this," Lando murmured in quiet amazement, as if only then realizing the full extent to which his ship, and his life, had been entrusted to the whims of a madman. "You're gonna get us all killed."

"No, I'm not," Han told him, "but we are going to need some help."

This is why you never let anyone fly your ship, Lando thought as he fought his way back to the lounge where the damaged remains of L3-37 were sliding across the floor next to the upended holotable. Outside, amid the frigid storm that Han had flown them into, the situation had gone from bad to worse—and then to something even beyond hopeless as they dodged debris and attack fire from the remaining TIEs that had followed them into the Maelstrom. Turbulence gripped the *Falcon* and shook it violently, and it occurred to Lando that if he failed in this simple task, he was effectively sealing their doom.

So don't screw it up, he told himself.

"Gonna need your help on this one, darling." Using his one good arm, he removed the shell protecting L3-37's brain module and extracted the neural core.

So far, so good.

He only hoped it would be enough.

Up in the cockpit, Han gauged their situation with a wary eye. Beckett was still firing, but the remaining TIEs swooped in tight, only getting bolder, committing themselves to the kamikaze mission they'd undertaken when they'd followed the *Falcon* into the Maelstrom.

"They still on us?" he asked.

"Like rashnold on a kylak," Beckett answered.

Han scowled. "I don't . . . know what that means."

"Like a ghingerson's pelt."

"Are they or aren't they?" Han shouted.

"Yeah, they—"

WHAM! A tremendous impact shook the *Falcon*, too

powerful to be a blast from a laser cannon. A massive hunk of frozen debris caromed off the side of the vessel.

"Watch where you're goin'!" Beckett shouted.

"Just hang on." Eyeing the floating obstacle course of carbonbergs in front of them, Han tilted the ship sideways and slipped between them, close enough that he could've sworn he felt them just scraping by . . . but somehow they made it. In the jump seat, Chewbacca let out an uneasy moan that managed to evoke both disbelief and nausea.

"Hey," Han told him, "lighten up. We're still alive, aren't we?"

"So far I'm not impressed," Beckett told him from the gun bay. "We're taking a real beating back here. Change up your game plan."

"He's right." Han glanced over at Qi'ra. "We need to divert auxiliary power to the rear deflector shield. Now."

"We sure do," she agreed.

"Qi'ra"—he looked at her again—"I'm asking you to do that."

"Right." She stared at the array of controls in front of her, moved toward one of them and hesitated, then shifted her hand to a different button. Then, aware of the way Han was staring at her: "Hey, we didn't all go to flight academy, okay?"

From behind her, a hairy arm reached over and moved effortlessly to flip a series of switches, adjusting the dial to divert power to the rear deflector shield. In spite of everything that was happening, Han turned and looked at Chewbacca in amazement.

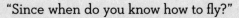

"Since when do you know how to fly?"

Chewie gave a quick moaning grunt. "I know how to do a lot of things. I'm a hundred and ninety years old."

"Whoa." Han blinked. "You look great."

He heard a crash in the lounge, followed by a sharp cry of pain and surprise. "Could use a hand back here!" Lando shouted.

Qi'ra looked at Chewie, then Han, aware of the effortless chemistry already between them . . . and the degree to which their survival, both immediate and long-term, depended on it. She stood up, vacating the copilot's seat.

"You sit here. I'll go help Lando."

Chewbacca sat down and immediately flipped on the freighter's headlamps, illuminating their way through the blizzard ahead. Han gave him a quick nod of thanks, and Chewie groaned back, "You're welcome." A moment later, the freighter shuddered with attack fire from the remaining TIEs.

"We gotta get these guys off our back," the Wookiee growled.

"I know, I know," Han muttered, and his eyes flicked to a massive hunk of carbonite hurtling toward them out of the storm. "Drop the landing gear."

Chewie stared at him. "Why?"

"I got a crazy idea. You trust me?"

His copilot groaned. "Not . . . really?"

"In that case, how about taking a leap of faith?" Han didn't wait for an answer. "It's a little something I learned from my pal Needles, best street racer in Corellia. Till he crashed and died, doing this. . . ."

The move, which some part of Han secretly doubted would work, brought them down hard on the surface of the carbonberg so for a second they seemed to be skimming along a vast obsidian floor at a dizzying rate of speed. Behind them, the TIE clung tight, guns spraying fire, moving in for the kill.

"This is your plan?" Chewie asked.

Han didn't answer. Behind them, the TIE was edging closer still, near enough that Han could almost feel the pilot nailed to the back of their ship. *Now*, he thought. The *Falcon*'s landing gear scraped and sprayed a sudden cloud of carbonfrost behind it to envelop the TIE, first blinding it and then freezing it completely, sending it spinning across the black surface, where it detonated in a brittle explosion.

"Nice work!" Chewie bellowed.

"Thanks, you too." Han shook his head with a dizzying sense of relief. "I gotta tell you, that's as close as I ever want to get to carbonite."

The Wookiee shrugged. "Yeah, I doubt you'll have to worry about it again."

"You ready?" Lando asked, and Han saw him and Qi'ra carrying L3-37's neural core and abdominal circuit board back into the cockpit.

"You got it?" Han asked.

Lando glared at him. "She's not an it!"

"Sorry."

"Just try to keep us steady, all right? This is precision work." Removing a panel of the navigational deck, Lando took out a penlight and began peering through a nest of wires while Qi'ra connected the circuit board she had extracted from L3-37's abdomen to the main terminal.

"Okay," Lando said, "now connect the T-line. Don't touch the magnet."

Qi'ra pressed the board into place. "I'm not touching the—" Sparks crackled and spat from the console, along with the scorched smell of hot copper. Ignoring them, Lando finished wiring the droid's neural core into the navicomputer and, upon making the last connections, sat back to wait for the system to reboot. The lights inside the cockpit flickered and came back on.

"She's interfacing. . . . She's part of the ship now," Lando said.

Han didn't look back. "How long until she can make the calculations for the jump to lightspeed?"

"Not until we're out of the Maelstrom," Lando said, "'cause the temporal distortion—"

"Yeah, yeah, we know."

And just like that, the turbulence stopped.

Everything stopped.

CHAPTER 18

"ARE WE OUT?" Qi'ra asked.

Nobody spoke. In the span of seconds, the *Falcon* had gone from a bone-rattling assault of TIE fighters, turbulence, and carbonbergs to a soundless, darkening haze that was somehow even worse. Lando consulted the newly upgraded navicomputer screen and shook his head. "I don't think so."

"Maybe we're dead," Chewie moaned.

"We're not dead," Han said. "Not yet."

"Elthree's online," Lando said. "Talking to the ship . . . and to me." The hopefulness of his voice faded as he gazed out the windshield, into the inky blackness that seemed to have draped itself around them endlessly in every direction. Without the stars or debris or *anything* to provide a sense of perspective, it was impossible even to know how fast they were traveling—or if they were moving at all. "Uh-oh," Lando said. "We're approaching the Maw."

"Doesn't sound like something we want to be approaching," Beckett said from the gun well.

A sudden flash of lightning burst in front of them. In that split second of illumination, Han glimpsed the void, the vastness in front of them, and the out-of-control velocity with which they were hurtling across it. Something tickled his skin, like the brush of a feather, and he looked down to see the small hairs on the backs of his arms standing straight up with static electricity.

"Um," he said, "you guys . . ."

Chewbacca was staring back at him, the Wookiee's fur completely on end so he looked like an enormous fuzz ball.

"What?" Chewie asked.

"Nothing," Han said. "Forget it."

"These ionic readings are spiking all over the place," Qi'ra said. "Like we're flying through some kind of electrical storm."

The power went out.

Plunged into blackness with only a strip of illuminated panel that cast an eerie glow across their faces, the cockpit fell quiet except for the rumble of the *Falcon*'s engines.

"Nice work, Han," Lando muttered.

"Hey," Han said, "I'm not the one who put in a flux regulator and a . . . minibar."

Chewbacca let out a low uneasy whine. "Don't like this."

"Okay, everybody just stay calm." Lando had his penlight out and handed a second one to Qi'ra. In the faint stream of light, she and Han set to work on the breaker box, detaching and reattaching wires in a frantic attempt to jump-start the *Falcon* back to life.

Han's heart rate quickened as he fumbled with the connections. Everything felt worse in the dark. With each passing second, the nebulous void outside the ship seemed to intensify, growing deeper, cloaking them in a claustrophobic silence. Getting chased by TIEs was better than this. He couldn't escape the sense that something was out there, looming in the blackness, just beyond their ability to see it.

"What's happening?" Beckett said through the comm. "How much longer?"

"Hang on, I think we got it," Qi'ra said, attaching the last wire. There was a sharp electrical pop and the lights inside the cockpit flickered and came on, the *Falcon*'s headlights blazing to life.

When Han looked through the front viewport, he saw they were flying toward a slick wet surface, like an enormous living wall, dead ahead of them.

"What is that?" Lando asked softly.

Nobody said a word. All at once the surface split open, skin peeling back to reveal the gelatinous orb of an enormous eyeball.

It was staring right at them.

Han wasn't sure who screamed first, but he knew that he *was* screaming, along with everyone else inside the cockpit. At the same time he was flying the *Falcon* straight down to avoid the thing—whatever it was—they'd just awakened.

"What are you doing?" Qi'ra shouted. *"What is that thing?"*

"Look out!" Lando yelled, and Han saw where they were headed. In an attempt to avoid the eye, which turned out to be a cluster of eyes, he'd flown straight down into something far worse—a swollen bulk of the thing's body, which was swimming with hundreds of writhing, electrified tentacles, each one covered with needle-sharp stingers. The tentacles were stretching out everywhere, grasping and clutching for the *Falcon*—he could practically feel them wrapping around the ship, working eagerly to dig out what was inside.

"This is the Maw?" he shouted.

"What?" Lando said. "No! This is a living—I don't know what this is, but it's not the Maw. I don't think."

"So the Maw is *worse* than this?"

"Well . . ." Lando's voice wavered audibly. "I think we're about to find out."

Up ahead, a warm amber glow spilled out of the darkness. From Han's viewpoint, the thing looked like a massive hourglass, a wormhole sucking in all the gas, dust, and debris and spitting it out into some other galaxy. With the creature they'd awakened coming after them and closing in fast, there was nowhere to go but straight into the Maw itself—and whatever lay on the other side. It didn't look promising. Behind them, the creature was coming closer, its mouth opening to reveal great daggerlike teeth.

He was aware that everyone on the ship was looking at him, waiting for him to make a decision that would either save them or doom them all.

No pressure, the voice inside his head said. *You're the pilot, right? Best in the galaxy?*

Suddenly, he knew what to do.

"Where's the . . ." he said under his breath, scanning the instrument array, and then he saw it. "Got it."

"Wait," Lando said, "that's my—"

Before he could finish, Han had hit the button to launch the *Falcon*'s escape pod. The pod shot free of the ship, and Han glimpsed it flying headlong toward the Maw as he gripped the yoke and pulled back as hard as he dared, skirting the edge of the wormhole. The tentacled creature surged toward them with ravenous strength.

All right, Big Ugly, he thought, *what's it gonna be?*

He didn't know for sure, but they were all about to find out.

CHAPTER 19

THE TENTACLED creature—a summa-verminoth by name, one of the great beasts of the Outer Rim, storied in galactic legend and lore—had lived out there for a long time. For untold eons it had drifted in silence at the center of the Maelstrom, in the loneliest part of the galaxy. Solitary but not alone.

Its beloved was there with it.

For the summa-verminoth, the wormhole known as the Maw was an enchantress, its great treasure, the culmination of all it desired. No matter how long the monster had gazed into her depths, the swirling, hourglass shape of the Maw's vortex had proven unfailingly mysteriously beautiful.

The verminoth had been drawn to her some untold period before, summoned there by a siren song it couldn't name, and it had remained, floating in space, not daring to progress any closer, yet unable to leave, sustaining itself with the various doomed morsels caught in her gravitational field. The Maw, in her infinite mercy, had allowed the creature to linger in her presence. So the two had struck up a strange coexistence, monster and void, until ultimately the verminoth could no longer bear the pangs of longing and had shut its many eyes in sleep, where dreams might provide the comfort it could not find in waking life.

Until now.

The intrusion of the metallic flying thing, that *insect*, had shocked the beast from its dream state. It had awakened hungry, angry, and miserable. The loneliness of its existence was as dreary as it always had been and stung all the worse from having gone on as long as it had. So much so that, beyond simple hunger, more than longing—

The summa-verminoth felt rage.

Chasing the metallic bug across the sky, sweeping its tentacles outward and opening its mouth, it permitted itself to be consumed by fury. Countless years of frustration and isolation, all bottled up for longer than even its ancient mind could remember, exploded out. It wouldn't just consume the flying metal object. It would *demolish* it. There would be no trace, not so much as a particle, to remind the galaxy it had existed.

Pulsing with wrath, the verminoth surged closer, jaws agape, preparing to bite down on its prey, when—unexpectedly—a second, even tinier metal piece shot out and went buzzing away from the bigger one. For a second, the great creature hesitated, confused by the new development. Somehow the smaller object was even more infuriating. Its very puniness embodied everything the verminoth loathed about its own circumstances—and worst of all . . . *the tiny object was heading right for the Maw.* As if it somehow had more right to join with her than the verminoth did.

Something like jealousy exploded through its brain, turning everything red.

Lunging headlong in its pursuit, venturing closer to the wormhole than it had ever dared go, the verminoth felt something it had never—in all its time there—experienced before.

The Maw was calling to it.

All the helpless longing the monster had ever felt for her was pouring back on it as she drew it closer, sucking it into her gravitational pull. This was what it had been waiting for all along: when in her depthless generosity, the Maw would fulfill both their destinies, accepting her admirer into her depths and transforming both of them forever in a mystical union.

With a great tremor of gladness, it went to join her forever.

From the cockpit, Han and the others watched as the tentacled thing flew toward the wormhole and was sucked in—first squeezed, then squashed, and then completely crushed, until it was flushed through the vortex of the Maw and was gone.

Han let out a breath of relief. "Well, I guess that takes care of that," he said, and then glanced back at the others. "Try to restrain your gratitude."

There was a quick electronic chirp from the navicomputer, followed by a series of digitized coordinates.

"Elthree's saying you want to go left," Lando said.

Han pulled the yoke. "Can't."

"What? Why not?"

"It's taking everything we've got to not get sucked into the Maw," he said. "We're stuck." He heard the ship creaking around them, its components shuddering and straining as the overburdened thrusters began to fail. "And now we're getting pulled backward. We don't have the power."

Qi'ra straightened up and glanced at him. "We do have power."

"It's not like I'm holding anything back."

"I mean . . ." She paused, thinking it through. "We've got enough coaxium on board to power a dozen Star Destroyers."

"Injecting it into the fuel line?" Han weighed the possibility and dismissed it with a quick shake of his head. "We'd blow up the ship."

"Not into the fuel line," Lando said, warming to her idea, "but if we put a single drop into the fusion reactor . . . it might give us the kick we need."

Beckett's voice came through the comm, where he'd been listening to the conversation. "I'm on it."

Han gripped the yoke tighter, to no avail. The ship's systems were all malfunctioning, and outside the viewport he saw pieces of the ship actually flying off, antenna arrays and other modifications swirling into the vortex. With every passing second, their window of opportunity was closing.

"Once we get lined up, it's gonna be a straight shot," Han

said. "As soon as that coaxium ignites we're gonna tear out of here, and the second we're clear of the Maelstrom we jump to lightspeed. Beckett?"

"Can't talk," Beckett yelled back over his comlink.

"Hurry up, we only get one shot at this thing!"

"Shut up and let me do this!"

Moments passed in tense silence. *Chewie was right,* Han thought. *We are dead.*

"Beckett!" he shouted. They were out of time. "I'm going to count you down! Three . . . two . . . one!"

"All right." Beckett's voice came through the comlink. "I'm ready! Now?"

"Now!" Han shouted back at him.

For a second, nothing happened—as if the only result of their desperate experiment had been to somehow snuff whatever energy remained in the reactor. In that terrible, seemingly endless interval of time, the ship was actually sucked backward, and Han thought all was lost.

Then it burst to life. The *Falcon's* thrusters surged forward with a sudden spray of blue fire, tearing the ship free of the Maw and throwing everyone in the cockpit hard against the nearest surface, and just kept accelerating.

"Left!" Lando shouted, pointing. "Even more left!"

"I'm working on it. Fair warning, Lando, if we get out of this, I don't think your ship's gonna look the way you remember it."

"As long as we get out of here alive, I don't care."

"I'm gonna remember you said that."

Beckett burst into the cockpit, clinging to the hatchway to keep from falling over. "Bad news. The canisters don't look good."

"How not good?" Han asked.

"They're cracking. Coaxium's getting more unstable by the second. I don't think we have much time."

"One crisis at a time," Han said. He saw the carbon-berg field thickening ahead, an obstacle course that would require all his focus and concentration. He swung the *Falcon* through the narrowest of escapes, so close that even he wasn't sure they were going to make it, and all the air leaked from his lungs in a slow hiss.

"Thought you were all talk," Beckett said, looking on with admiration, "but you are a heckuva pilot."

"Thanks. Just wish Captain Almudin was here."

Chewie moaned. "Who?"

"He's the one who kicked me out of the flight program."

"So you could show him what he missed?" Qi'ra asked.

"No," Han said, "so he could die with us when those canisters explode." He looked at Lando. "Hyperspace coordinates set?"

"The destination, yes," Lando said, "but I can't enter a starting point. I don't know exactly where we are."

"You better take an educated guess." Han's eyes flicked from the pulsing alarms of the instrument panel to the view in front of him, where massive sheets of carbonite continued to shift and grind and collapse into each other. "The second we're out, we gotta jump. Otherwise—"

THOOM! A massive carbonberg, the biggest yet, tumbled in seemingly out of nowhere and collided with the *Falcon*, slamming it sideways, knocking the ship far off its trajectory. Chewbacca let out a startled bark of dismay. When Han glanced over at Qi'ra, he saw that she was gazing back at him.

"We're gonna die, aren't we?" she asked matter-of-factly.

He didn't respond, then turned to Chewie, picking up on the nearly telepathic communication the Wookiee had conveyed with a slight grunt. "Yeah," he said, his voice low. "I see it, too, pal."

It was straight ahead of them, almost too small to be seen, a slender crack between two carbonbergs and a sliver of black space and stars—their one way out of the Maelstrom. Even as Han watched, the 'bergs began collapsing into each other.

We're never going to make it.

Yeah? another voice in his head answered. *Since when does that mean you don't try?*

"Lando!"

"Ready!" Lando said.

"Chewie, when I tell you, kick out the thrusters and jump to lightspeed."

Qi'ra stared at him in disbelief. "What are you—"

"Remember the alley we squeezed through in the Santhe shipyards?"

"Yeah, I remember it *didn't* work!"

"This time it's gonna."

"Blaze of glory, huh, kid?" Beckett shook his head. "I just wanna say it was nice knowing all of you."

"One . . ." Han focused on the narrow slit between the carbonbergs. In his peripheral vision, he saw Chewbacca place his hand on the lightspeed lever, his eyes on Han.

The Wookiee growled. "Hope you know what you're doing."

"Two . . ."

Han felt Qi'ra's hand on his shoulder, her fingers digging into the muscle, and cranked the *Falcon*'s yoke hard, as far as it would go, tilting the ship on its side. "Punch it!"

They shot forward in a headlong burst, Han's grip locked on the controls, skimming through the impossibly narrow slit between colliding carbonbergs and squeezing free at the last possible second. Clear space opened up around them, Chewbacca hit the lever, and the *Falcon* jumped to lightspeed. The stars elongated around them until they streaked back what looked like forever in all directions, and then, with a breathtaking rush of pure velocity—

Gone.

CHAPTER 20

THE GRIZZLED OLD AIR TRAFFIC controller on Savareen had spent all day up in the tower, marking time as he stared across the white dunes of the Pnakotic Coast and the Emerald Sea beyond it, lost in thought. As scenery went, the sweeping coastline was certainly better than the tower's alternative view: the long-decaying industrial buildings, tanks, and fuel pipes of the refinery.

He'd done his time down at the refinery, but those days were long gone, and now he intended to spend the rest of his life, however much remained, reclining up there in relative peace and quiet, until—

"Savareen tower!" a voice crackled through the antiquated radio, wavering in and out but unmistakably urgent with near panic. "This is the *Millennium Falcon*. We have the coaxium, but it needs to be offloaded immediately, and— hang on . . . what?" There was a chorus of other voices in the background, all talking at once, followed by the man's voice again, sounding more panicked than before: "That's what I'm telling him! Like *immediately*!"

The controller leaned forward and began to tap out his response.

"We're here now!" the man's voice cut in. "I see you!"

There was a sudden roar and the entire tower shook on its foundations, rattling the windows and forcing the controller to grab his radio console to keep from falling off his stool. Out his window he saw the ship go hurtling past and settle on the landing pad outside. Switching his attention from the vessel to the refinery behind him, he started to tap out a new message.

Send help. All you've got.

The offloading went like a dream.

Han figured the old fossil in the control tower must have jumped on the horn for reinforcements without delay, because when the ramp went down, the Savarian workers were already waiting to move the coaxium into the rusty pipes running to the main refinery. Helping move the final canister into place, Han turned to the worker and pointed back up at the *Falcon*.

"See that ship?" he said. "She just made the Kessel Run in twelve parsecs."

The worker paused momentarily, stone-faced and clearly skeptical, and Chewie growled: "Actually, it was more like thirteen."

"Not if you round down," Han said, and walked over to Lando, who was looking up at his baby with visible anguish. The ship looked nothing like it had when they'd left Vandor. Running the gauntlet had ripped off all her precious added adornment, leaving a stripped-down, mean-looking freighter covered in dents and scrapes.

"Yeah." Han put his arm around Lando. "She's one heck of a ship."

Lando stared at him coldly. "I hate you."

"I know."

The smuggler shrugged off Han's arm. "I'll be in *my* ship," he seethed. "In *my* quarters. Waiting for *my* cut of the money. After which, I never want to see you again."

"Never?" Han asked, but Lando didn't answer.

Neither one of them noticed the small blinking device, caked in carbonfrost, attached to the *Falcon*'s landing strut. If they had, they might've recognized it for what it was, although it was unlikely they could've guessed how long it had been there.

An Enfys Nest homing beacon.

Han gazed up the hillside, toward the decrepit-looking refinery perched atop the dunes. Even from a distance, the factory was menacing, its pipes spreading out in all directions like the legs of a biomechanical spider that might jump out of the sand at any second. It was the perfect workplace for a people who, as far as Han could tell, were physically incapable of cracking a smile, maybe for fear their faces would fall apart.

"Not too friendly, are they?" he asked.

"They ain't paid for their congeniality, kid," Beckett said. "Come on."

They started up the dunes, followed by Qi'ra and Chewbacca, the sun pounding down on them as they climbed, the arid wind like heat from a blast furnace. Halfway up,

Han looked back and saw that Qi'ra had found a spigot and was drawing water, washing her hands and splashing a little down the back of her neck. Watching her, he couldn't keep from glancing at the Crimson Dawn brand on the inside of her wrist, and he thought again of how they'd started all this, what already felt like a very long time before.

"So," he said, "where's your boss?"

"He'll be here."

"Then what?"

"You delivered." Her voice, Han thought, had become the coldest thing on that overheated planet. "You'll get paid, buy your ship."

"That's not what I'm asking," he said. "What I mean is—"

"I know what you mean." Qi'ra turned to squint out at the sea. "That can't happen."

"'Cause you're with Dryden?"

"I'm not *with* him, but I do owe him. He helped me out of a bad situation, and . . ." She drew in a breath, and in that brief interval of silence, Han heard all the unspoken tension of the time they'd spent apart. "He's been good to me."

"And how long do you have to pay that back?"

"Everybody serves somebody, Han. Even Dryden Vos."

"Hey—" he started, but she cut him off.

"Trust me, you do not want to make an enemy of Crimson Dawn. And that's exactly what we'd both be doing if I left here with you."

Han's jaw tightened. Hearing her say those things, even the way she pronounced the name of the cartel with a respect that bordered on fear, triggered something inside him, a mixture of anger and defiance. "I'm not afraid of Dryden or Crimson Dawn. You saw what happened back there. I can handle myself. I'm not the kid you knew on Corellia, not anymore."

"No?" she asked. "Then what are you?"

"I'm an outlaw."

She smiled at that and couldn't seem to keep herself from laughing a little.

"What?" Han frowned. "I'm not kidding."

Qi'ra raised her hand to touch his cheek. The tips of her fingers were still damp from the water she'd splashed over her neck, and they traced the contour of his face, cooling the heat that the sun had stamped against his skin.

"Okay, outlaw," she said, "tell yourself whatever you want. But I just might be the only person in this galaxy who knows what you *really* are."

"Oh yeah?" he asked. "What's that?"

She smiled again, but it was different this time, without irony.

"You're the good guy."

"That's"—he blinked at her, unsure what to make of that assessment—"wrong. No. Definitely not the good guy. I'm a terrible human being. And I'm prepared to do whatever's—"

"Hey!" Beckett cut in as he and Chewbacca trudged up the slope past them. "They said when the coaxium's ready, we'll collect it up there."

When Han looked back at Qi'ra, she'd already started walking away.

The good guy, he mused, following her the rest of the way up to the refinery. What was "good" supposed to look like in a profession as morally bankrupt as his? Even his best intentions had been recklessly improvised half measures that usually only made things worse for himself and his friends. And the scrapes he somehow *had* managed to get them out of—most of them, anyway—well, Han had to admit, at least in the privacy of his own mind, that it had been mainly due to luck.

But not *just* luck.

Even Beckett had said he was a heckuva pilot, hadn't he? The memory of those words, the grudging note of respect in the midst of everything that had been going wrong, brought a smile to Han's face. Gradually, the smile faded.

Being a good pilot, or a good thief, or whatever . . . didn't mean he was actually *good*, not the way Qi'ra had meant it. Did it?

So what was it exactly that she'd seen in him that he didn't see in himself?

And what did it mean that she saw it there still?

Shaking his head, baffled by the implications that he couldn't yet begin to wrap his head around and maybe never would, Han turned back to the hill and kept climbing.

———

There was a kind of makeshift canteen set up just outside the refinery, its roof and walls long before caved in, with large woven blankets spread overhead to block the oppressive glare of the sun. Women and children sat in the shade near a row of dusty windows, hunched in the shadows and sipping from mugs. A handful of workers were gathered on their break, across from a counter with a lone attendant whose face didn't change as he watched Han and the others approach.

"Hear you make a mean brandy," Beckett said to the attendant, and held up four fingers, one for each of the party.

"And water," Qi'ra added, taking her place next to Beckett. "Please."

But the man didn't move to serve them, and Han saw him staring back at Beckett with that same expressionless gaze. Han scowled. *What now?* The man's stare moved to the entrance behind them before returning to Beckett . . . and Beckett, for his part, seemed to realize what it meant, because his shoulders drooped with weariness, and he turned with resignation and finality to walk back out onto the stretch of sand from which they'd come.

"What's wrong?" Han asked. "Where are you going?"

Looking behind them, he stopped talking.

The sand, which just moments earlier had been empty, was occupied by twelve masked marauders like the ones who had attacked them on swoop bikes in the Iridium Mountains of Vandor.

Standing in front of them, face covered by the familiar bone mask, cloak rippling in the breeze, was Enfys Nest.

CHAPTER 21

FOLLOWING BECKETT OUT on the sand, Han started to reach for his blaster and heard Beckett say, "Don't."

Han stopped and put his hands in the air slowly. His mind was reeling, trying to process the new development. How had Enfys Nest known to find them on Savareen? Not that it mattered, ultimately, but after everything they'd been through, the Maelstrom and the monster and the Maw, not to mention the heist itself, to have Enfys Nest and the Cloud-Riders show up like that—the shock left him stunned and furious.

"You must've known you'd see me again," Enfys said through the mask's voice-modulating filter.

"I was countin' on it," Beckett told the marauder. "Just didn't plan on it being so soon is all. Of course now you've got a problem—"

"Big problem," Han said. Beckett turned to look at him, but Han ignored it and plowed ahead, the bluff taking shape in his mind as he spoke. "You happen to notice that freighter down by the water?" he said, pointing down at the *Falcon*. You know what's on it? About *thirty* hired guns. All I gotta do is give 'em the signal"—he snapped his fingers—"and you're surrounded."

Enfys said nothing for a moment. All at once, a roaring sounded overhead, shaking the air above the refinery, and everyone in the party stopped and looked up to see the *Millennium Falcon* go hurtling past. Han felt a brief flash of hope when he thought Lando might actually be coming for them—but the ship just kept going, streaking off into the sky to vanish completely, abandoning them. The echo of its engines seemed to linger a long time before finally dwindling away to silence.

Han closed his eyes. *Lando,* he thought darkly. *Thanks a lot, pal. If I ever run into you again*... Pushing the thought aside, he opened his eyes, took three steps back, and looked back to Beckett. "Sorry, you do your thing."

Beckett turned to Enfys. "By the time that coaxium's refined, Crimson Dawn will be here. So go ahead, kill us; they're just gonna kill you."

"Hang on," Qi'ra said. "Maybe there's a compromise that doesn't involve so much killing."

"Yeah," Han put in. "We should at least explore other options."

"Save your breath, kid. They're marauders. Pirates. They don't care what or who they destroy." The bitterness in the older man's voice, Han realized, the low growl in which he spat out the words, was a direct reaction to all that Enfys and the others had cost him already, not just loot but lives: Rio and Val. Rio had been a friend and fellow soldier, and Val much more. "All they know how to do is kill."

No one moved. Han watched Beckett, right hand at the ready, waiting to see what was going to happen. If the shooting started, he meant to at least take out a few of the marauders, as many as he could. They wanted the coaxium? Fine, but they would pay for it, the steepest price there was.

But instead of shooting or ordering an attack, Enfys did something totally unexpected, reaching up slowly and deliberately to remove the bone mask.

Han stared at the face that had been concealed beneath it. He'd expected a battle-scarred outlaw, some hideous alien species, even a renegade droid—anything but what he saw.

The teenage girl gazing back at them had curly auburn hair and brown eyes that, even at first glance, seemed to go on forever. Nobody else moved as she made her way calmly across the porch, the planks creaking audibly as she went to lean against the wall and then turned to gaze up at the ruins of the old refinery. Her face was luminous and almost angelic, but beneath it lay a deep sense of fatigue, a terrible heaviness, as if she'd seen and done far more than anyone her age ever should have endured.

"I need a drink," she said. "Bring them inside."

Inside the makeshift canteen Enfys, glass in hand, spoke again, her voice refreshed but no less haunted.

"My mother once told me," Enfys said, "about a band

of mercenaries who came to a peaceful planet. They had a resource there that these men coveted, so they took it. They kept coming back, taking more, till finally the people resisted. When the ravagers returned demanding their tribute, the people shouted back in one voice"—an abrupt coldness flashed across her expression, her eyes going to ice—"'No more.'"

Enfys looked at Han, who realized that he was staring at her, riveted. Regardless of her age, there was something compelling about the young warrior, a charisma as powerful and potentially unstable as the coaxium itself.

"So they cut the tongue out of every last man . . . woman . . . and child," she said softly. "That was many years ago. Do you know what that pack of animals became?" She turned to an old woman who had been sitting behind them with a cup in her hands, listening to the story along with everyone else. "Tell them."

The old woman gazed back at Enfys for a moment, then dipped her finger into her mug and used it to draw on the dusty window behind her, making a straight line with a semicircular sun rising above it, exactly like the brand on Qi'ra's inner wrist.

The symbol of Crimson Dawn.

Chewbacca let out a low moan of dismay. Next to Han, Qi'ra's face tightened as she struggled to absorb this information, to make it fit with everything she knew about her employer and the man who'd been her master.

"That's just one story," Enfys said. "Crimson Dawn and the rest of the Five Syndicates have committed unspeakable crimes all across the galaxy."

Beckett grunted, sounding unconvinced. "Says you."

"No," she said. "Says *them*."

Han looked behind her, his eyes widening as one by one, the Cloud-Riders removed their helmets and masks. Every one of them, he saw, was a different species, each from a different homeworld ravaged and exploited by the sinister partnership between the powerful syndicates and the Empire. Among them, Han recognized the red-skinned face of a Mimbanese National, like the ones he had faced as an Imperial mudtrooper—and a knot rose in his throat. These faces, these individual beings, gave silent testimony to the savagery and corruption of an organization that would stop at nothing to fuel its own unquenchable greed.

"Each of our worlds has been brutalized by the syndicates," Enfys said. "Crimson Dawn will use their profits from the coaxium that you stole to tyrannize system after system. In league with the Empire."

"And what would you use it for?" Beckett asked.

She regarded him coolly, as if she had anticipated that question. "The same thing my mother would've used it for if she'd survived and still wore the mask—to fight back." She made a fist at her side. "We're not 'marauders.' We're allies," she said, then paused, the slightest ghost of a smile passing over her face, an expression of hope, "and the war's just beginning."

Beckett's gaze was locked with hers, and Han couldn't read what was going on behind it in response to everything she'd said, but the old gunfighter's face appeared visibly changed, as if he was seeing things in an entirely different light.

Then he turned and walked away.

Han made his way across the sand in the opposite direction, stopped, and squinted up at the sun.

Up until then, when confronted with authorities and injustices above his pay grade, it had been simple enough to remind himself why he was doing the job. Getting paid, getting himself a ship, and getting out as quickly as possible. If Chewbacca or Qi'ra wanted to be part of that plan, fine, he'd be glad to have them . . . but ultimately, there was only one opinion that mattered, and it was his. Qi'ra herself had summed it up well. *Somebody falls, you keep running. It's how you stay alive.*

That settled it, then.

He was an outlaw, with an outlaw's creed.

Simple enough.

Looking across the sand, he saw that Chewbacca had gone off on his own, about fifteen meters away. The Wookiee was hanging his head in silence, clearly still ruminating on Enfys's story.

As Han watched, one of the Savarian children who had been sitting in the shade of the awning leapt to her feet and ran toward Chewbacca. The girl's mother—seeing only a monster and her daughter's impending death—stood up with a wordless cry of warning, but the girl ignored her completely. She scrambled over to Chewie and tugged on the fur of his leg, beaming up at him with eager delight. Han couldn't tell what she was saying, but the message was clear enough. She'd found a new pet.

Han watched as Chewbacca reached down and, with great gentleness, lifted the girl into his arms. He saw the smile on the girl's face, and this time it wasn't Qi'ra's voice he heard in his mind but Enfys's.

We're allies, and the war has just begun.

CHAPTER 22

HAN FOUND BECKETT standing on the ridge of a dune with his back to the refinery, gazing out at the sea, silhouetted against the distant expanse of green and blue. Han could tell from the way the old gunfighter's shoulders straightened that he'd heard him approach, but Beckett didn't bother to turn around, even when Han stopped walking and broke the silence.

"We can't give the coaxium to Dryden Vos."

Beckett turned unhurriedly to regard him, one corner of his mouth twisting upward.

"You joining the cause, Han Solo?"

"Just trying to make it out alive," Han said, which was, he supposed, partially true. It was the part of the truth that would make most sense to someone like Beckett, anyway.

"Got a plan?" Beckett asked.

"You think I'd come up here without one?"

"Doesn't answer my question."

"I've got the beginnings of one," Han said. "A way to get our money, get out from under Crimson Dawn's thumb..." He couldn't resist adding: "And put Dryden Vos out of business."

"And maybe get your girlfriend back while you're at it, huh?" Beckett asked, but the smile on his face was cynical, the grimace of a man who had made a lifetime of questionable choices and faced hard consequences as a result. "Let me tell you something, kid. You do not tangle with Dryden, 'cause unlike us, he actually *does* travel with hired guns, his own private army of enforcers."

Han glanced over his shoulder, where Enfys Nest watched them from a distance, her image wavering in the sunbaked air that rose from the dunes.

"So does she," he said.

"What do you think they're saying?" Enfys asked.

Qi'ra stopped in her tracks. She'd been walking toward the girl without a word, but Enfys had sensed her there without so much as a backward glance. Qi'ra looked over at Han, watching him explain something to Beckett, and knew without a doubt what Han was saying.

"He's gonna try to help you," Qi'ra said.

Then Enfys did turn to lock eyes with her. "And you?" she asked, her pupils sharp and piercing, glinting in the harsh sunlight. "You're with us, too?"

Qi'ra didn't answer for a moment. She was aware that Enfys wasn't the only one listening. Chewbacca was standing within earshot, his head cocked, awaiting her reply. Her thoughts cycled back almost involuntarily to Dryden Vos, to everything he had done for her, good and bad, since she'd entered his service years earlier. It had been a cruel apprenticeship. She had spent her life trading one form of indentured servitude for another, a fact that Dryden knew as well as she did.

Enfys was still looking at her, waiting for her answer. Qi'ra moistened her lips and replied with as much confidence as she could muster. "Yes. I'm in."

Enfys's expression didn't change. With a curt nod, she turned and walked away.

When Han had finished explaining his idea to Beckett in as much detail as he could provide, he stood back and awaited his mentor's verdict.

"Dicey," Beckett said at last. "Lotta ways it could go south."

"That's why I need my partner."

"You come up with a perfect plan, there's a hundred ways it could go wrong. If you can think of ten of 'em, you're a genius. And, kid, you're no genius."

"But it's still not bad," Han said. "Are you in?"

Beckett looked down at the dusty tips of his boots. When he raised his head again and ran his hand through his hair, there was a shadow over his face, and Han couldn't make out his eyes. "Not this time," he said. "I'm leaving. You want out, you should come with me."

Han just stood there, momentarily speechless. He'd always known that Beckett was in it for himself, but somehow hearing him say so out loud, that he was leaving them on their own after coming so far—it felt like abandonment.

"I thought you didn't believe in running," he said finally.

"I prefer it to dying." Beckett saw the disappointment on Han's face and let out a slow breath. "Aw, come on, kid, don't be sore. . . ."

"I think you know I'd do it for you," Han said, the words out before he could stop them.

Beckett shrugged. "I'm a lot smarter than you are." He glanced past Han and over to Enfys, meeting her eyes. In the interval of silence, something passed between them—the old gunfighter forgiving her for the loss of Val and Rio while Enfys, in turn, allowed him to walk away unscathed—and then Beckett turned and started down the slope. At the last moment, seeming to remember something, he turned and looked back at Han.

"If by some miracle you happen to make it out of here," he said, "find me on Tatooine."

"What's on Tatooine?" Han asked.

"Heard about a job, some big-shot gangster putting a crew together." Beckett nodded, mulling over the opportunity. "Yeah, that'll be the one."

"The one?" Han asked.

"My last score. Still got debts to pay before I can go back to Glee Anselm and learn to play the valachord."

Han couldn't help smiling. Young as he was, he recognized a pipe dream when he heard one, just as he knew the necessity of the story that Beckett would continue to tell himself. It would be there as long as he needed it, whether it proved to be true or not.

"Good luck, Beckett."

The old gunslinger nodded and headed down the lonely windswept path. The westering sunlight blazed around him, shimmering across the green surface of the sea, and Han wasn't sure if Beckett glanced back at him one last time or not before he disappeared from view.

CHAPTER 23

"WHAT?" CHEWBACCA GROWLED. "What are you looking at?"

"Nothing," Han said, shaking his head. "You just look different, is all. I guess I just got used to seeing the whole, you know . . ." He gestured across the Wookiee's chest, indicating the place where the bandolier had been just a few minutes earlier. Chewie had taken it off, and he almost looked naked without it.

Chewbacca moaned unhappily, visibly displeased with its absence. "Trust me, I know how you feel," Han said, glancing down at his own empty holster. "But this is how we gotta play it if we're gonna get this right. Trust me, okay?"

Chewie gave him a sidelong glance but said nothing. They were standing outside the gangway to Dryden Vos's star yacht, the luxury vessel docked and gleaming in front of the decrepit refinery like some galactic economist's study in contrasts. It hadn't taken Dryden long to get there. He'd been waiting for their signal and was more than ready to receive his part of the deal.

"All right, let's do it." Han grabbed one of the two absurdly heavy suitcases, grunted, and set it down again before Chewbacca reached down without a sound and picked up both of them. With Q'ira behind them, they stepped aboard the yacht.

It was darker in there and blessedly cool. Han waited for his eyes to adjust to the diminished light. After a moment he recognized the familiar weapons-check attendant behind the counter on the opposite side of the alcove that also served as the elevator. The attendant gazed at them as Qi'ra unbuckled her holster and handed it over.

"Welcome home," he said. "The boss'll be happy to see you."

"Thanks, Toht."

The attendant glared at Han and Chewbacca, his expression hardening. "I'll take your weapons."

"Didn't bring 'em," Han said, and nodded at the empty holster. "Didn't seem necessary for a friendly business meeting."

Toht leaned over the counter, eyeing the holster, and did a similar check on Chewbacca before turning his attention to the suitcases. Qi'ra gave him a quick nod, letting him know that it was all right, and the attendant waved them past. The door shut behind them, enclosing them in a soft but unmistakable silence.

As the elevator rose, Han gazed out the windows at the desolate dunes and the refinery behind them, as dreary and hopeless a place as the galaxy had to offer. The winds blew mean on Savareen. If things didn't go as planned, this place would be their burial ground.

Then it's your job to make sure it goes right, he thought, and turned his attention to Qi'ra. She, too, was looking out at the desolate landscape, her expression bleak, like a condemned prisoner on her way to the gallows.

"You all right?" he asked quietly.

She just nodded, eyes still far away.

"It'll be over soon."

"I know it will," she said.

"And we're gonna win."

"It's not that kind of game, Han. The object isn't to win, it's to stay in it as long as you can."

He frowned at the darkness in her tone, not what he'd expected given how readily she'd gone along with his idea. "You don't know everything."

"No," she said, "just a bit more than you."

The elevator stopped moving, and Chewbacca moaned. "Get ready."

The doors opened.

"Here they are."

Dryden was seated behind his desk as they stepped into his study, and he rose to greet them with a smile and open arms. He was dressed more casually than the first time Han had seen him, shirt collar unbuttoned, sleeves rolled halfway up his tanned and muscular forearms, demeanor relaxed for the informal reunion with his old friends. Behind him, outside the windows, solar flares streaked and burst across the sky above the sparkling Emerald Sea.

"You know," Dryden said, "my men told me, 'No way they pull this off.' They said, 'Qi'ra's too inexperienced.' But I believed in you. I had—" He stopped, a line of puzzlement creasing his forehead. "Where's Beckett?"

"Beckett didn't make it," Qi'ra said.

Dryden's face went blank for a second as he registered the news, and then his expression darkened with what appeared to be genuine grief. Stepping closer, he put one arm around Han's shoulders and the other around Qi'ra, literally coming in between them as he drew them close, his voice sad but understanding.

"Tell me."

"Job took a bad turn," Han said. "He died . . . saving my life."

Dryden nodded eagerly, the sympathetic listener. "How are you holding up?"

"Me?" Han glanced at him. "I'm . . . okay."

"Good," Dryden said, patting him on the shoulder. "That's good. Losing colleagues, never get used to it. Never. Still, life goes on." Then, abruptly, his voice brightened. "Colo claw fish, anyone?"

Something stirred next to Han and he jerked his head sideways to see that one of Dryden's enforcers had seemingly materialized out of nowhere, startling him. The enforcer was holding a tray of slimy-looking raw fish, the glistening bodies so fresh that they were still wiggling on the plate.

"No, thanks," he managed, and his gaze traveled across the study to a second enforcer, who stood motionless against the wall, holding a multibladed Bundki cutlass. Together, the two enforcers made a silent but unmistakable statement: it would only take a few sweeps of that cutlass, and Han and the others would look an awful lot like what was squirming around on that plate. He swallowed and tried to muster an appreciative glance. "We just ate."

"Whatever Beckett's shortcomings may have been," Dryden continued, apparently oblivious to his guest's revulsion, "I always admired him. He had principles, and when he made a commitment, he honored it." He beamed at Han and Chewbacca, ever the gracious host. "I think we can all take solace in knowing he would've been happy you're here, following his example."

"We learned a lot from him," Han said honestly, and Chewie echoed the statement with a slightly more ambivalent-sounding moan as he put down the cases of coaxium.

"Han and Chewbacca behaved . . . admirably," Qi'ra said. "They'll make reliable smugglers should we have need, as soon as they get a ship."

"Gotta have one of those!" Dryden exclaimed, a little too enthusiastically. He took a seat on the couch and patted the cushion beside him, indicating for Qi'ra to join him.

"We'd appreciate the opportunity to work for you again," Han said.

Dryden, for his part, was still lavishing all his attention on Qi'ra. "You know, my dear, I would've been inconsolable had anything happened to you." Reaching up, he ran his fingers over her cheek like a man appreciating a lovely piece of art, savoring its beauty, while Han forced himself not to react. "I have no one in my life that I trust the way I trust you."

"Yes, well . . ." She gave him a tight smile. "That's very nice."

Han cleared his throat. "So I guess we'll just take our payment and be on our way. I'm sure you have markets to dominate, competitors to crush. . . ."

Dryden snapped his head around, giving Han a bloodless smile. "First let's see what you brought me."

"You want me to open it?"

"Yes, Han." The other man's face showed no hint of expression, his voice eerily emotionless. "I really do."

With a slight cock of his head and a little shrug, Han reached down and unlatched the lid of the case. There was a sharp hiss of escaping steam as the seal broke, and he removed the lid completely, setting it down on the floor beside him before reaching in and bringing out a rack of coaxium vials. The vials clinked together softly, the unmistakable glow of the coaxium illuminating his face as he displayed them for Dryden.

"Give me one," Dryden said.

Han hesitated. "I don't think that's a good idea. It's pretty unstable."

Dryden's voice went cold. "I never ask for anything twice."

Seeing that he had no choice in the matter, Han lifted a rack of vials and handed it over. Dryden received it eagerly and held it up for closer inspection, the glow reflecting in the intense blue of his eyes.

"Magnificent," he said softly. "How'd you do it?"

Han shrugged. "Wasn't easy."

"No," Dryden said, "I mean . . . it looks *exactly* like the real thing."

Something tightened in Han's chest, like a steel fist clenching his heart. He was aware of everyone in the room—Dryden, his enforcers, Qi'ra, and Chewbacca—all looking at him, waiting to see what he'd do next.

"That's because it *is* the real thing," he said.

"And I'm saying I'd believe you," Dryden told him. "It's *that* good. . . ." Then his expression *did* change. Han saw the elegant features twisting ever so slightly to betray the emotion rising beneath them. "Had my associate not warned me about your little plan to steal my money and give the *real* coaxium to Enfys Nest."

He dropped the tray of vials on the table in front of him with a clunk.

"I must say, I am very . . . *very* disappointed."

Nobody breathed. The tension in the room was so thick that Han felt as if he could almost see it coloring the air between them, giving everything the same reddish hue that was rising to spread over Dryden's cheekbones. Han's eyes flicked to Qi'ra, then back to their host, and he realized that he was talking again, the words coming before he'd even had a chance to think them through.

"Listen, Dryden, I don't know what you think or what Qi'ra told you but I would *never* even *dream—*"

"Not Qi'ra." Dryden sprang up from the couch, his neck and shoulders straightening as he shot to his feet. "No, Qi'ra, it seems, has a weakness for you. We'll get to that in a moment. I'm talking about my *other* associate."

Walking past Han to the desk, he pressed the intercom button.

"Won't you join us?"

On the opposite side of the room, the elevator opened, and another man walked in.

It was Beckett.

CHAPTER 24

"SORRY, KID."

Beckett's blaster was in his hand, pointed at Han and Chewie. Seeing it, Han let out a low, scarcely audible groan. It was the sickening feeling of stepping forward in anticipation of solid ground and instead plummeting into empty space. For a long moment Han didn't speak. Then, finally, he managed: "Why?"

"Hey." Beckett pursed his lips, clearly uncomfortable with the betrayed look on Han's face—uncomfortable enough, anyway, to try justifying his decision. "Enfys took everything I cared about. I'm not giving her anything. And Dryden's my friend. I wouldn't betray him! Also . . ." He shrugged, and finished with the obvious: "It's a lot of money."

"That it is," Han said.

"Kid, you didn't pay attention. I told you not to trust *anybody*."

Han's eyes darted over to the lid of the coaxium case, and he'd already decided to move when he heard Beckett's voice cut in. "No, no, no, step away from that," he said, and turned to Han and Chewie. "Keep your paws where I can see 'em."

One of Dryden's enforcers, the one who had been stationed across the room with the cutlass, walked over to the lid. Reaching in, he pulled out the DL-44 blaster Han had stashed inside it before they'd entered. Nobody—least of all Dryden himself—looked remotely surprised to see it there.

"It's too late," Han said, resigned to whatever was going to happen next. "The coaxium's refined. Enfys has it."

Beckett nodded. "Figured she might."

"So," Dryden said, "I've sent my people into the refinery. They'll collect your friends, bring them back here"—he sighed at the inevitability of what came next—"to see their masks added to my collection before they die."

Han shook his head. "They'll never—"

"Kid," Beckett said. "They already have."

"What . . . ?"

"Just wait."

Han didn't say anything. Seconds passed, time seeming to stretch in the quiet room as Dryden peered out the yacht's circular gold windows, his hands clasped behind him in a posture of one who didn't mind waiting. After what felt like forever, there was a click and a voice came over the yacht's intercom.

"It's over, sir," an enforcer reported. "We've got 'em, and we've secured the package."

"Excellent." Dryden's casual tone was that of a man acknowledging a foregone conclusion. "Thank you, Aemon." He walked back over to where Qi'ra was sitting and looked down at her as if from some great distance. "My heart is broken, it really is. What would you do if the person you trusted most betrayed you?"

Dryden actually seemed to expect an answer, and Qi'ra gazed up at him. When she spoke, Han could hear her weighing every word carefully, as though her life depended on it. Which, he thought, it just might.

"I'd want to know why she did it," Qi'ra said. "If it was a moment of weakness or something else . . . and then I'd ask that person to prove their loyalty by sacrificing"—her eyes flashed to Han—"something they love."

Beckett shook his head, lips upturned in a wistful smile. "Warned you about her, too. It's a shame, we would've made a great team."

Han let out a long, slow breath. "You're wrong about one thing, Beckett. I was paying attention. You told Chewie that people are predictable." Staring right up at Beckett, he smiled. "You're no exception."

Before Beckett could reply, the yacht's intercom activated again, but this time it wasn't an enforcer's voice that came through the speaker.

It was the sound of blaster fire.

And battle cries.

And screaming.

CHAPTER 25

"–EMPTY!" the enforcer was yelling from the other end of the comlink. "The case is empty, it's a—"

The words ended with a shriek of pain, and the intercom fell abruptly silent.

"Aemon?" Dryden's expression of smug self-assurance drained away, leaving his face looking strange and defenseless, almost childlike in its surprise. "What's happening? Come in!"

"I think he was gonna say, 'It's a trap,'" Han said. He looked at Dryden, frowning slightly with mock concern at the unexpected turn of events. "You didn't send *all* your fancy enforcers, did you? 'Cause that would leave you"—he pointed at the two in the room, counting them off—"a little shorthanded around here."

Beckett was staring at him, eyebrows slightly raised, and Han gave him a little two-fingered salute off his temple. His mentor couldn't seem to help smiling, shaking his head at how well the kid had learned. Then something occurred to him, and he turned his attention to the rack of glowing vials on the table, where Dryden had unceremoniously dropped them.

"Which means the *real* coaxium . . ." Beckett began.

"Leaves here with one of us," Han said. "Uh-huh."

He waited, watching Beckett make the calculations in his head, wondering how long it would take him to get there.

It turned out to be not long at all.

Beckett's hands were a blur, twirling his blasters out, firing both at the same time. He shot the enforcer with the fancy cutlass across the room, blowing him back against the wall, and the other enforcer with the platter full of fish, the whole slimy mess flying as he went out the window with a scream.

"What are you *doing*?" Dryden shouted, his voice splintering with panic.

"Thinking," Beckett said, "and I prefer to be the only one with a blaster while I'm doin' it." He nodded at Han. "You can put that back in the case. Nice and easy."

Han hesitated only a moment, then lifted the tray of vials and placed it as delicately as possible back in the case. He put the lid back on and fastened the clasps.

"That's better." Beckett pointed one of the blasters at Chewbacca. "You're comin' with me, big guy."

The Wookiee let out a low groan, and Han nodded in sympathy, thinking, *You and me both, buddy.*

Chewie lifted the coaxium cases, Beckett motioning him toward the elevator with a blaster. Across the room, Han saw Dryden's face boiling over with rage that could no longer be restrained.

"Some friend," he spat.

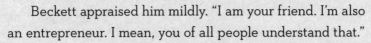

Beckett appraised him mildly. "I am your friend. I'm also an entrepreneur. I mean, you of all people understand that."

"You're making a horrible mistake."

The old gunslinger seemed to consider it for a moment, then shrugged. "Could be," he said. "Won't be my first."

"It'll be your last."

"Maybe, maybe not. Don't be so negative." Beckett followed Chewbacca into the elevator, one blaster pointed at the Wookiee's back, the other trained on Han, Qi'ra, and Dryden. "See you around."

The elevator door closed and Han thought, *Do it now*.

He snapped into action, leaping forward and sliding across the polished floor of the study toward the fallen enforcer who'd taken his blaster. It was still there, tucked under the body, the guy's hand still warm. Sitting up, pivoting, leveling the blaster, Han saw—

—Dryden, faster than Han could've imagined, ready for him. Dryden was holding something that looked like a combination brass knuckles and double-edged laser blade that he'd taken from the rack by his desk.

Han pulled the trigger. Dryden ducked and rolled across the floor behind a display case as shattered glass rained down on his head. There was a brief silence, followed by the sound of shifting debris, and then Han heard the other man's voice, as smooth and cultured as ever, drifting up from behind a partially demolished suit of ancient Mandalorian armor.

"Han, I think now's as good a time as any to reevaluate our relationship."

Han crouched low, heart pounding. "Yeah?"

"What do you say we join forces, go after Beckett together?"

"Yeah," Han said. "Let's definitely do that."

He sprang up to fire and recoiled in shock. Dryden was standing there, less than a meter away. The blades slashed with unfathomable speed and precision, forcing Han backward across the litter of broken glass and artifacts.

"Teräs Käsi." Dryden, for his part, seemed to be enjoying himself. "I've become something of an enthusiast of it."

"That's really wonderful."

Dryden was moving again, eliminating the distance between them, the attack coming faster than Han could process. A kick, a punch, a flip, the blows arriving in a flurry of stabs and bursts. Pain exploded in the side of Han's skull, the room already spinning. Dryden's left foot flew up and Han's right wrist went numb to the fingers.

Whatever you do, don't lose the blaster.

He looked at his hand and saw it was already gone. As Dryden leapt into the air, no doubt intent on flattening Han's windpipe with both feet, Han groped out blindly, managing to find the broken spear of some ancient warrior who'd probably never dreamed his weapon would be called into service under such circumstances. He swung it up and blocked Dryden's move, clubbing him sideways but barely slowing him down. The guy was a force of nature.

Scrambling backward, Han dove for his blaster and went into a tuck and roll, ending up behind one of the couches. Dryden's voice was as conversational as ever.

He's not just enjoying himself, Han thought, *he's having the time of his life.*

"You can't win," Dryden said. "Even if you do, you'll be looking over your shoulder the rest of your life."

"I'm kinda getting used it." Han took a deep, centering breath. His thoughts went back to the conveyex job, that moment standing in the open gantry of the AT-hauler when it had been time to jump, and he whirled around to open fire—

—and instead saw Qi'ra. She was flipping through the air, landing in front of him. Something flashed in her hands—the multibladed Bundki cutlass that had been in the possession of Dryden's enforcer. She knocked the blaster away and then tossed Han aside with an almost offhand demonstration of strength before whipping the cutlass around to point the tip of the sword at his heart.

Han stared up at her, unable to speak.

"I'm sorry," Qi'ra said.

"You must understand, Han." Behind her, Dryden was stepping back into view, advancing toward them. "She's done things that you don't know anything about, but I do. I know everything." His face was calm, the dispassionate expression of a man stating a simple fact. "Once you're part of Crimson Dawn, you never leave."

He was closer, standing directly behind Qi'ra. In the interval of silence that followed, Han glanced at the brand on Qi'ra's wrist, the mark that would always be there, could never be removed.

"It's not true," he said quietly. "I *know* you."

She nodded, eyes gleaming, on the verge of tears. Over her shoulder, Dryden leaned in, his voice not much more than a whisper.

"Prove it to him," he murmured. "For me."

"It's what I was taught," Qi'ra said, her eyes never leaving Han's. "How to find my opponent's weakness and use it. And today . . . I'm yours."

She spun around, slashing with the cutlass, slicing open Dryden's shoulder. Dryden jerked backward, genuinely startled, the laser blades flashing to deflect her assault with a series of quick thrusts and swipes. He was more practiced, but Han glimpsed something else in Qi'ra's eyes, a brutal ferocity, a soul-deep determination, at all costs, to eliminate anything that might stand in her way.

Dryden lunged again, the dagger getting wedged in the gap of Qi'ra's sword. For an instant they stayed like that, locked and immobile, the silence of the room seeming to vibrate around them. Then Han heard her snatch in a quick breath before she swung the whole thing into Dryden's chest with a single, unhesitating stroke, impaling him on the edge of his own blade.

Dryden's eyes widened, fixing on Qi'ra with shock . . . and something else, too, Han realized. Something like love.

"Yes," he managed, and was gone.

CHAPTER 26

"I HAD TO DO IT," Qi'ra said simply.

Han nodded, still stunned, watching as she lowered the blade and allowed Dryden's body to sink to the floor, taking its place amid all the demolished finery. "Yeah, no," he managed at last. "I mean . . . you did, and you *did*."

She walked over to him. "Beckett and Chewie. You have to go after them."

"Right. What are you gonna do?"

She glanced at the display case of crown jewels, their beveled edges gleaming faintly against crushed velvet, reflecting untold depths. "If we're going to give all the coaxium to Enfys, we'll need something to buy our ship with."

"*Our* ship?"

She nodded, and Han realized he'd been waiting his whole life for this moment, and as vivid as it all was—the smell of smoke and scorched fabric, the chaos, the spilled blood, and the thudding of his own pulse—it felt almost too good to be real, a conversation that could only be happening in his dreams. "You mean—"

She kissed him. Her lips were soft, lingering on his as

if to prolong a moment she knew couldn't last. Han felt her hand on his cheek, the warmth of it on his skin, and opened his eyes.

"Qi'ra . . ."

"Save Chewbacca. He needs you." She gave him a sidelong glance. "And you're gonna need him, too."

He knew she was right, but he found himself hesitating, not wanting to leave her.

Get moving. It's not going to get any easier.

Tearing himself away, he ran to the elevator and turned to look back at her through the open door.

"Smile," she said.

"What?" He frowned, but her eyes were sparkling, brimming with all the radiance, courage, and intelligence he'd loved about her since they were kids.

"That's the word that I couldn't think of before," she said. "Whenever I imagine myself off with you, on some adventure, it always makes me smile."

Say something, idiot. Tell her how you feel.

"Go. I'm right behind you," she said. The door closed, and she was gone as the elevator began its descent.

The ride down seemed to take forever. Han tried to make sense of everything that had just happened, but he couldn't seem to get past that kiss and the promise she'd made of the ship they'd have together—the *life* they'd have . . . as soon as they put Savareen behind them.

When the door opened on the gangway level, his eyes went automatically to the weapons-check window. The attendant's body lay facedown, dangling halfway out of the window, and the bodies of his assistants were sprawled around him. Beckett had taken care of them on his way through—of course. At that point, Han expected no less.

Stepping over the bodies, he ducked through the main hatch and walked down the gangway, back into the brightness of day.

The Emerald Sea stretched out in front of him, glinting on the horizon. Shielding his eyes, he gazed over the bluffs until he caught sight of the figures trudging down the coastline. Beckett and Chewie were still far enough ahead that they wouldn't see him coming. Not yet, anyway.

By the time he got to the beach, he was running.

After Han left, Qi'ra stood over the jewel case for a moment, gazing down at its contents. The gems were like stars, she thought—compelling and brilliant, full of promise for those seeking a new life, but distant, too, in a way that could prove misleading and ultimately heartbreaking. Nobody owned them, not permanently, and in the end they would outlive all their admirers.

Such was the nature of beauty.

Such was the nature of power.

She turned from the case and crossed the study to where Dryden's body lay lifeless, face tilted upward, eyes glassy and fixed on nothing. Kneeling down, she grasped his hand in hers. She wondered if she might feel something, touching him one last time—if not a sense of loss then perhaps just relief or uncertainty about what lay ahead. But the cold hand triggered no emotional response in her. It was like picking up another artifact, a lifeless object, nothing more.

She slipped the Crimson Dawn ring from Dryden's finger and let his hand drop. Walking over to the desk, she inserted the ring in the communicator and turned it like a key.

Something in the room changed.

The face that appeared above the desk was one she'd only glimpsed once before in her life. It was fearsome red, marked by a series of complex black tattoos, the scalp crowned in an array of horns that protruded directly from the skull. His presence before her, even as a hologram, made her take a step back, though she was careful to maintain eye contact. Showing respect to the leader of the Crimson Dawn crime syndicate was crucial, but showing weakness would be dangerous.

He stared at her, awaiting her report.

"I regret to inform you that Dryden Vos is dead," Qi'ra said, "murdered by the thief he hired to steal the coaxium shipment, his friend Tobias Beckett."

Maul's face remained neutral. "Where is the shipment now?"

"Gone. Beckett took it, slaughtered the others. I alone survived."

The Zabrak appeared to contemplate her news in silence. Then: "One man could not do this alone."

"I wasn't there. But if I had been, perhaps I could have saved him."

Maul considered this. "For now, you will assume control over all of Dryden's territories and interests."

"I appreciate your faith in me," Qi'ra told him. "I won't disappoint you."

The smile on the leader's face was tight, a thin razor slash. "Bring the ship and come to me on Dathomir. You and I will decide what to do about the traitor Beckett and his accomplices."

"I'm on my way."

"And, Qi'ra?"

She looked up at him.

"He always spoke highly of you."

"Thank you," she said.

"He loved you," the leader said. "But also, I suspect, feared you a little."

"Feared me?"

"You were his favorite. Of all his disciples, he said you were the only one with the potential to surpass him. You and I will be working much more closely from now on."

"I look forward to learning all I can from you," she said.

CHAPTER 27

THE SUN WAS SINKING below the Emerald Sea, solar flares bursting above, when Han finally caught up with them. From his vantage point in the dunes, he had a clear view looking down on Beckett and Chewie as they approached the weathered one-seater ships that were apparently Beckett's intended escape route from Savareen. Not that such things mattered anymore.

It was time to finish this.

He crept closer, edging down the embankment until he was close enough to hear the sound of their footsteps in the sand.

Ten meters away.

Five.

Han drew his blaster from its holster in absolute silence and aimed it at an invisible point between Beckett's shoulder blades.

"Stop."

The old gunslinger whirled, blasters out and ready, and froze, seeing the barrel of Han's own blaster at point-blank range. He smiled and shook his head.

"You're relentless, kid, I'll give ya that."

Chewie moaned loudly and set the suitcases down in the sand, edging away from the standoff. "What, did you take the scenic route?"

"I came as fast as I could, buddy," Han told him.

Beckett's gaze hadn't wavered, both his blasters still trained on Han. "Dryden dead?"

Han nodded.

"Qi'ra kill him?"

Han blinked, startled by his mentor's insight. Beckett saw his reaction and seemed unable to keep from shaking his head at his former pupil's relative innocence.

"You still don't get it, do you?" Beckett asked. "It was never about you. She's a survivor."

A surge of anger rose in Han, tightening his throat. "You know what your problem is? You think everybody's like you."

"Not you, kid. You're not like me." Beckett made a slight adjustment with his own blasters, his fingers tightening almost imperceptibly on the triggers. "I hope you're still paying attention, because I'm about to tell you the most—"

Han pulled his own trigger, and the blaster leapt in his hand. It was so unexpected that for an instant Beckett simply stood there, unable to register what had happened. Then, lowering his blasters, he looked down at the wound in his gut with an expression of shock, followed by understanding.

He fell. Han went over and knelt beside him, the light already departing from the older man's eyes. "Beckett . . ."

"No." Beckett bit his lip, in almost too much pain to bear but determined to speak. "You made the smart move, kid. For once. I would've killed you." His breathing was already becoming labored, and Han saw that he'd finally released his grip on the blasters that had seemed so utterly at home in the gunslinger's grasp for so long. The weapons slipped away and fell into the sand beside him, which was already turning red with Beckett's blood.

"Kid?"

Han took Beckett's hand and squeezed it, looking into the weathered eyes, letting Beckett finish.

"I really was gonna learn to play that valachord. . . ."

Han nodded. "I know you were."

Beckett laughed, scarcely more than a breath that seemed to get caught in his lungs. A stillness swept over him, like the shadow of an object falling fast, and then whatever it was that had made him Beckett, whatever had given him life and uniqueness and mystery, was gone. The beach was silent except for the distant thunder of the waves.

Han gazed down at the dead gunslinger. Was this what was waiting for him, too, someday? Some unsung ending on a remote beach somewhere in a remote part of the galaxy? There were worse ways to go. He found himself thinking of his own father, whose life had been a slow, drawn-out series of defeats and concessions to forces he'd never understood. The man whose body lay before him had lived and died according to his own rules without giving a centimeter, right up to the end. When death came for him, Tobias Beckett had gotten the last word.

A rumbling sound rose from the far side of the dunes, shaking Han from his thoughts. He stood and climbed the crest of the bluff, squinting as Dryden's star yacht rose into view, the curve of its hull cutting against the sunset.

Han shaded his eyes with his hand. He could just make out the figure standing inside the viewport.

It was Qi'ra.

She was smiling.

Han stared at her, motionless. Although it should've been impossible to see from that distance, with the sun streaming behind the yacht, he was aware of the sadness in her smile. He felt it in his chest like a physical ache, the knowledge that she'd chosen her career over him and that those promises she'd made—promises he'd wanted so desperately to believe—had been as empty as the cases Dryden's enforcers had tried to take from them back at the refinery. Even as she'd spoken the words, she'd known they were lies.

Feeling more alone than he ever had in his life, he closed his eyes and felt a hand on his shoulder.

He turned and saw Chewbacca standing alongside him. The Wookiee moaned softly, and Han met his friend's sympathetic blue eyes.

"Thanks, buddy," he said, and drew in a deep breath, looking down at the suitcases as if noticing them for the first time. "You're right. Let's finish this."

From her place on the catwalk of the refinery, Enfys Nest watched Dryden's star yacht rising higher, the vessel pausing to bank in the sky before its thrusters ignited and it vanished forever.

"I knew he would betray us."

Enfys recognized the voice as belonging to Benthic Tubes, a Tognath marauder who had accompanied her to Savareen. Benthic stormed off, kicking one of the bodies of Dryden's fallen enforcers on his way out.

She looked around, meeting the wary glances of her other allies, all of them expressing the same sense of uncertainty. They had followed her because they had trusted in her cause . . . but what about the people she'd put *her* faith in?

Then she saw a Savarian child, a girl no more than four or five years old, turn her head to look at something in the distance. The child lifted her hand to point at whatever had caught her attention.

Enfys walked down from her post to join the girl, both of them looking out toward the dunes, into the amber light of the flaring sun. Two silhouettes were walking toward them, one much larger than the other.

One of them was carrying suitcases.

Later in that long, long day, as he watched Enfys and her allies secure the real coaxium cases to her swoop bike and get ready to ride away with them, Han Solo tried not to think

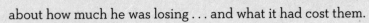

about how much he was losing . . . and what it had cost them.

But it was no use. The bitterness of it lingered.

Enfys finished her work and approached him, seeming to read his thoughts. She nodded at the cases, strapped in place and ready for transport. "Do you know what that really is?"

"Yeah." He didn't bother trying to soften his tone. "About sixty million credits' worth of refined coaxium."

"No," she said. "It's the *blood* that brings life to something new."

"Yeah? What?"

She met his gaze and held it. "A rebellion."

Han shook his head. Big words, he thought. Politicians' rhetoric. He'd believe it when he saw it.

"You could come with us, you know," Enfys said. "We need warriors, and leaders, like you."

Han listened to the words, wondering if they truly applied. Warriors. Leaders. For a moment, so brief that it nearly passed without his noticing, he weighed her offer. Then he shook his head again and laughed it off, wondering what he'd been thinking.

Enfys didn't appear to be particularly surprised by his decision. "Maybe someday you'll feel different."

"Don't hold your breath, kid."

She reached into her pocket and handed him a small glowing vial. Han saw that it was coaxium . . . the same size as the one he'd traded for his freedom back on Corellia what felt like a thousand years before. After regarding it for a moment, holding it up to what was left of the setting sun, he turned and handed it to Chewbacca.

"Don't lose this."

Enfys surprised him by laughing out loud, the happy laughter of a teenage girl, and then impulsively throwing her arms around him.

After a moment of hesitation, he surprised himself by hugging her back.

CHAPTER 28

NUMIDIAN PRIME WAS a backwater planet whose sweltering jungle outpost would never enjoy a brisk tourist trade. To those criminals, fugitives, and degenerate gamblers who arrived seeking safe haven, the jungle cantina provided temporary shelter, a place to hide from whatever was hunting them before they left again and tried to forget they'd ever darkened its doorway.

That made it perfect for Lando Calrissian.

He was poised at the Sabacc table behind a mountainous pile of chips, feeling absolutely at home. Drink in hand, flirting with the Twi'lek gambler next to him, he was about to place another bet when he became aware of a sudden silence at the table and two figures looming over him.

One of them was extremely . . . tall.

Lando stood up, a big grin on his face. "Han . . . Chewie! You're *alive*. That's great!"

"What, you mean after you left us for dead on Savareen?" Han narrowed his eyes. "I should have Chewie pull your arms out right now. In fact—"

Chewbacca moved threateningly toward Lando, who recoiled. "Han! Come on, we're friends!"

Han glared at him and then, after a long moment, stepped forward and threw his arms around Lando, embracing him.

"I got you! You should've seen your face." Still hugging Lando, clapping him on the back, Han deftly removed the spare card he'd known would be in the hidden sleeve holder and palmed it before releasing his grip on Lando's arm. "Admit it, you really thought he was gonna pull your arms off."

"No," Lando said, "I knew you were kidding." He settled back down at the table, relaxing. "So, you bring my cut?"

"Your cut?" Han gaped at him. "We barely got out of there alive! All we walked out with was this." He nodded at Chewie, who held up the coaxium vial. "Figure it's worth about ten thousand, enough for a decent stake."

Pausing, he took a look around the table at the ill-tempered, menacing gamblers hunched over their cards. Lando noticed the glint in his eye and smiled charmingly.

"You want a rematch?"

Han thought of the card he'd lifted from Lando. Without needing to look, he knew that it would be the green sylop. Hands at his sides, careful not to avert his attention from Lando's face, he slipped the card into his own sleeve, smiled, and shrugged.

"Why not?"

There were as many different accounts of that marathon Sabacc game as there were players at the table that evening. Each of the gamblers told their own version, each emphasizing a different facet of the story. What all of them could agree on was the final moments when Han and Lando faced off over an enormous pile of money in the middle.

"I'm telling you," Lando warned him, "don't do it. You fold now, you walk away with almost enough to buy your own little ship." He sat back. "You call, I'm gonna clean you out again."

"I dunno." Han seemed to take a long time considering his cards. "I'm feeling pretty lucky tonight. Think I'm gonna call."

"You really got it bad for the *Falcon*, huh?"

"Trust me, it's mutual. She loves me."

Lando shook his head, the expression on his face evident enough. You couldn't argue with stupid. He perused his cards again . . . and his smile faltered.

Han watched it happen, allowing himself to enjoy every second. He could visualize Lando's finger feeling around inside the cuff of his sleeve, checking the mechanical clip for the green sylop, and finding it empty.

Han cocked his head, the very picture of innocence.

"Got everything you need, pal?"

"Sure." When Lando's smile returned, it was a sickly version of itself as he spread his cards out on the table, revealing a solid hand.

"Not bad," Han said. "Not bad at all. If only you had this . . ."

He moved his right hand ever so slightly to reveal the

pilfered green sylop between his fingers, feeling the weight of Lando's incredulous stare.

"You woulda been able to beat this," Han finished as his left hand tossed his cards out on the table to reveal—

Full Sabacc.

The crowd erupted, Chewie cheered, and Han Solo sat back with a grin, folded his hands behind his head, and savored the moment for all it was worth.

He figured he'd earned it.

EPILOGUE

"FEELS GOOD TO BE BACK."

Settling in behind the yoke of the *Millennium Falcon*, Han took a moment to hang the gold dice above the control panel, then sat back and regarded them momentarily with a pang of loss. The ache was still there, but it already wasn't as bad, and he had every reason to expect that at some point it would fade completely. Meanwhile, there were more pressing matters to focus on. He turned to the copilot's seat, where Chewbacca had already taken his position as first mate and was looking at Han expectantly.

"Where to?" Chewie asked.

"Tatooine," Han said. "Beckett said he heard about some gangster putting together a job."

The Wookiee's response to their destination planet was a less-than-enthusiastic moan.

"No, I'm tellin' ya, it's gonna be great, and when have I ever steered you wrong?"

Chewbacca shook his head but seemed to know better than to argue. He rested one hand on the lever, activating the thrusters and awaiting the order for takeoff.

The *Falcon* came to life around them. What Han had told Lando back at the cantina hadn't been a lie or even an exaggeration. He loved this ship, and the ship loved him back.

Some things really were that simple.

He glanced at Chewbacca and felt the Wookiee's blue eyes looking back at him with perfect understanding—the way that he'd wanted to be seen by Beckett and Qi'ra. He realized now that he'd found his true partner. What more could you ask for?

"Punch it," he said.

And like that, they were gone.

ABOUT THE AUTHOR

JOE SCHREIBER is the author of many books for adults and young readers. He lives in California with his family, a poodle, and a rabbit named Captain Holly.